The Quiet Heart

Rae Simons

Heartsong Presents

A note from the Author:
I love to hear from my readers! You may write to me at the following address:

Rae Simons
Author Relations
P.O. Box 719
Uhrichsville, OH 44683

ISBN 1-55748-623-9

THE QUIET HEART

"You look pretty tonight, little Dorrie."

"Thanks." *Not exactly a conversation opener*, she thought. The coffee finished brewing, and she poured them each a cup.

Liam took his cup and came to stand beside her where she leaned against the kitchen counter. She could feel his warmth very close, his shoulder brushing hers, but she felt tense and on edge. She looked into his face, and at last she could stand the silence no longer. "You were wonderful with Clem," she said softly.

His mouth twisted. "She wasn't exactly receptive to what I had to say. Not that I blame her."

"She's just so sick right now. But I know she'll appreciate what you said when she feels better."

Liam shrugged.

"I never thought before about what you said," Dorrie continued, "about her being afraid to marry Mason because of what happened to your parents. But it makes sense."

Liam sipped his coffee.

"I mean," Dorrie said, "the death of your parents at such a young age had to affect her psychologically. Both of you." She looked again into his face.

He smiled. Then he reached and took the coffee cup from her hand and set it on the counter behind them. "Shh, Dorrie," he said and pulled her into his arms.

Dorrie stood with her face against his beard, feeling awkward and breathless. After a moment, he turned his head and his lips touched hers, gently first and then more deeply.

"Oh, Liam," Dorrie said when at last they drew apart, "I love you so much."

RAE SIMONS is the pen name of a new, gifted, inspirational romance author. Rae has spent several years editing and proofreading the works of other authors, but this is her first published novel. Rae and her family make their home in New York.

one

Her new home looked nothing like she had expected. Dorrie
Carpenter sat in her car staring at the sagging line of the
roof, at the unpainted clapboards. The tiny house stood
alone on the empty country road, surrounded by a grove of
oak trees; it looked quiet and unused. Dorrie rolled down
her window, trying to catch the sound of a neighbor's lawn
mower or a child's voice calling, but the only noise was
the wind whispering in the oak leaves overhead.

The stillness rang in her ears. For the last eight hours,
during the long drive from her parents' home in southern
Pennsylvania, she had traveled in a steady stream of song
and prayer, listening to tapes, and talking out loud to God.
"The other drivers will think you're a crazy woman if they
see you talking to the air," she had told herself, but she'd
been too excited to care. She was on her way to her new
job in upstate New York, and she knew a whole new life
was waiting for her.

Clem, her roommate from college, had found this house
for the two of them to rent. Clem had already begun her
nursing job at the town clinic, and Dorrie soon would be
starting her first teaching position at a nearby Christian
children's home. Dorrie felt as though she had been buzzing in circles, whirling with excitement for weeks, as she
had gotten ready for the trip here.

And now here she was at last. She opened her car door
and stood up, stretching her long arms and legs. The quiet

seemed to settle over her like a blanket. She shifted her shoulders and frowned, longing for a sound to break the stillness.

"You don't like it. I can see it on your face."

She whirled toward the voice. Clem stood at the edge of the field beyond the oak trees, her arms full of goldenrod and purple asters. Beneath her short, yellow curls, her small, round face was rosy and full of dimples, and Dorrie smiled, thinking she looked like a child in some old-fashioned illustration.

"It's just so quiet here," Dorrie said. "I'm used to the city, remember? And I *was* wondering if that roof will keep out the rain. Not to mention the wind and snow." She laughed and ran to hug Clem. "I'm so glad to see you—I don't care what the house looks like. I know it was all we could afford. And like I told Mom, now that we're sharing a house, we'll soon be saving a bundle just on our long-distance phone bill. No more two-hour phone calls every time you and Mason have a fight." Clem rolled her eyes, and Dorrie laughed. "So come on. Show me the place."

Inside, the house had a bedroom for each of them with a large kitchen-living room in the middle. A braided rug was on the floor, and patchwork pillows were plumped high on the deep sofa and chairs.

"The truck with your stuff came last night," Clem said, pointing to the sofa and chairs, the round kitchen table that stood in one corner, and a stack of dishes still wrapped in newspapers. "My brother came over last night, and he and Mason lugged everything inside and helped me arrange things. The bedrooms are just alike with the same view, so I didn't think you'd mind not being here to fight with me over who got which. Mason and Liam set up your bed, and they're bringing mine later today."

Clem reached for a glass jar from the cupboard beneath the sink and filled it with water. She pushed the gleaming flowers into it and set it on the center of the table. "There. It's starting to look like home already, don't you think? You'll have to tell your mom how much I appreciate her letting us use your grandmother's old furniture. The place would be pretty empty otherwise."

Dorrie flopped down in one of the overstuffed chairs and looked around. "Where did all the homey touches come from, though?" She looked at the braided rug and hand-sewn pillows, the ruffled curtains and the glowing pictures of English cottages that hung on the walls. "Don't tell me you had all this stuff in your old apartment. My place at graduate school was a veritable hole—dark and dreary with plastic furniture that had belonged to the landlord, and a torn yellow shade over the only window. I kept meaning to make it look nicer, but I was hardly ever there, I was so busy. But this—this is a real home. This is wonderful." She picked up one of the patchwork pillows and hugged it to her.

Clem smiled. "It is nice, isn't it? Despite how it looks from the outside. Gram sewed the pillows and curtains herself. And the pictures are from her attic. She says she remembers them from her mother's house when she was a little girl. Do you like them?"

Dorrie nodded. "They're perfect. And what about the rug? Is that from her too?"

Clem shook her head. "We have my brother to thank for that. He said it never went with the rest of the stuff in his apartment, and he thought it looked like something we would like."

"That was nice of Liam." Dorrie tried to keep her voice casual. "And it was nice of him to put in a good word for me at the children's home. Who knows if I would have gotten the job there if he hadn't worked there already." She picked up the end of her long red braid and studied it, as though she were searching for split ends. "So how is he these days?"

A shadow flickered across Clem's face. "Liam's all right. So far as I know. It's just—oh, I don't know. The same old thing I used to tell you back in college. He says all the right things—but I always feel his heart isn't really behind his words." She sat down in the other chair and curled her legs under her. "You know, Dorrie. Growing up with Gram and Grandpop, what with Grandpop being a pastor and all, the church was as much our home as the parsonage. I used to feel I was being soaked with God's presence, it seemed such a constant thing. After Mom and Dad died, that atmosphere of love and prayer healed me. But with Liam it was different, maybe because he was older. I could feel him pulling into this hard, tight shell. The shell was a nice, shiny one, but the real Liam was hidden away inside it. It was like—oh, as though he were learning the language of a foreign country, while shutting out the very heart of that country's culture. He knows the right things to say, but I'm not sure he knows Christ."

Dorrie's hands clenched the soft pillow. Clem's brother Liam was the one subject she and her friend had never agreed on. She forced her hands to relax and said lightly, "Come on, Clem. After spending the summer with my own sister and brother, I know how easy it can be to see your siblings' faults. I'm sure they could see mine as clearly as I did theirs'. But that doesn't mean we doubt each other's commitment to Christ. We understand we're still all too human, that God's still working on us."

Clem shook her head. "That's not what I mean about Liam. If anything, he's *too* perfect. Not humble enough, maybe. I never hear him talk about needing God's help with this or that. Oh, I don't know how to make you see." She looked at her friend's face and sighed. "You still feel the same way about him, don't you? That's what worries me."

Dorrie's cheeks burned. She tried to laugh. "I don't know why you should worry. It's not as though he's ever tried to sweep me off my feet."

Clem sighed again and pushed the short yellow curls off her forehead. "Well, I wouldn't mind if he did, you know; if I could be sure things were right between him and God. You two are the people I love most in the world."

"What about Mason?"

Clem blushed. "Him, too, of course. But he is definitely *not* sweeping me off my feet. Here we've been dating three years, ever since our senior year at college, and we're still not engaged. And now—" She looked down at her hands and frowned. "You remember how last summer he visited that friend of his who's a missionary in Colombia? Well, now Mason says he thinks God may be calling him to the mission field, too. He's all excited about translating the Bible into native languages."

"So?" Dorrie looked at Clem's face. "Why should that make you sad? Missionaries get married. And you loved South America that year we went as summer missionaries after our sophomore year. So what's the problem?"

Clem got to her feet. She straightened a picture, pushed the ruffled curtains back from the window. "No problem," she said at last. "Except that he's never even mentioned marriage. I could use my nursing down there. Before Mason even mentioned the mission field, I was wondering if that's where God was leading me. You know me. I love other countries, I love learning new languages, and I love —" She leaned closer to the window, her face hidden.

"And you love Mason," Dorrie finished for her.

Clem laughed, but her voice was muffled, and she kept her face turned away. "Except that he makes me so mad sometimes. But I can't imagine not being with him, not seeing him. I guess I really just wish things could stay the way they are between us. I sense that he's feeling restless—and that scares me." She took a deep breath. "And speaking of which, here he is now." She turned away from the window and ran a quick hand across her eyes. "Liam's truck just turned down our road. The two of them must be here to deliver my bed."

Dorrie's stomach clenched with excitement, and her hand went to her hair. She tried to smooth the wisps that had come loose from her braid. Clem laughed. "You look fine. More than fine. Beautiful, in fact." She followed Dorrie to the door and hugged her quickly. "I'm so glad you're here, Dorrie. Whatever happens with Mason, I know it will be easier now that you're here with me."

Dorrie returned the hug, but her eyes went over Clem's shoulder to the small pickup that bounced up the dirt road to their new home. On the passenger side she could see Mason's square face and short sandy hair, and beyond him— She took a deep breath, trying to still the trembling of her heart.

The truck pulled in their driveway and stopped behind her car. The doors slammed. "Hey, Dorrie, you still driving that heap of junk?" Mason called.

Dorrie grinned and nodded. She looked past Mason and met Liam's blue eyes, as blue as the sky beyond them, she noticed. His dark hair was a little shorter than the last time she had seen him, but it still had the same black gleam as a crow's feathers. He had grown a trim beard that emphasized the line of his jaw, and the hair on his face was a shade lighter, more brown than the hair on his head. She hadn't seen him for more than two years, not since her college graduation, and she felt now that she would never be able to look at him long enough to make up for those long and empty years. Her eyes moved from his face to his muscled shoulders beneath the navy knit shirt he wore, down to his khaki pants, noticing each detail, feeding on the sight of him.

"Hi, Dorrie." At the sound of his voice, her eyes leapt back to his face, and she blushed. He smiled. "I've missed you." Something inside her heart seemed to leap out of place, leaving an empty hole behind. She swallowed hard.

"I've missed you too," she murmured, hoping he wouldn't hear the quaver in her voice.

She watched while he and Mason unloaded the pieces of Clem's bed frame from the back of the truck. "Just let us get this set up," Mason said over his shoulder, "and then we're taking you two women out for pizza. We figure Dorrie needs to relax after her long drive."

❧

Later, hoping she didn't have tomato sauce on her chin, Dorrie watched Liam as he talked with Mason. She thought his beard made his dark, narrow face look like a French courtier's; she was fascinated by the way his slim fingers moved, folding and unfolding a paper napkin. She smiled dreamily, then caught Clem's frown and dragged her attention back to the conversation.

They were discussing their jobs, she realized. Mason was a youth pastor at the same church that Liam and Clem's grandfather still pastored, while Liam was the athletic director at the Christian children's home where Dorrie would soon be teaching.

"When do you start work, Dorrie?" Mason asked, his mouth full of his fifth slice of pizza.

"Next week."

"We're awfully glad to have you," Liam said. "The children need someone who really knows the Lord."

Dorrie glanced at Clem. See, she wanted to say, how can you say this man isn't right with God? "I'm excited," she said out loud. "And nervous too. I did my student teaching back in college, of course, and then I did an internship at a pediatric psychiatric hospital as part of my master's program. But this will be my first experience actually being on my own with a group of kids, responsible for them for an entire day." She met Liam's blue gaze and faltered, shaken by the attentive interest she saw there. "Tell me something about the kids, Liam," she managed to say, glad to have a reason to stop talking and merely watch his face.

Liam shrugged. "They're a needy bunch. Most of them from broken homes. The reason they're at the Home is because they've run into trouble either at home or school—or both. Either the state child protective agency or the local school districts pay for most of their boards and tuitions." His eyes were on the paper napkin between his fingers; he folded it into an accordion, unfolded it, folded it again. "There's about three times as many boys as girls—and they don't have a lot of manners. You'll have your hands full, I have to say, Dorrie." He looked up then into her eyes, and he smiled. "But with the training and experience you've had, I know you can handle them, Dorrie. I have confidence in you. That's why I recommended you so highly to our administration."

Once again, Dorrie felt her face glow.

&

"What was with you and Liam tonight?" Mason and Liam had gone home, and Dorrie stood in the doorway of the tiny bathroom, watching Clem wash her face. In the mirror, Clem looked at her above the washcloth.

"What do you mean?" Dorrie asked.

"You know." Clem's voice was muffled by the cloth. "All those long, warm gazes the two of you kept exchanging. Is something going on I don't know about?"

"How could something be going on? The only time I've even talked to him in the last two years was when you suggested I call him about the job at the children's home. I never even saw him when I came up for the interview." Dorrie remembered the dark disappointment she had felt, and smiled, knowing now that God had been in control all along. She shrugged her shoulders, trying to hide from Clem the certainty she felt inside. "He was just being friendly."

Clem shook her head. "I've seen that look on Liam's face before." She hung up the washcloth, then turned back to her friend. "Liam's good with women. He likes to make them fall in love with him. But he never gets serious, and the women always get hurt. Believe me, I've seen it happen before." She frowned and shook her head. "Oh, Dorrie, your face is so easy to read. First, you were jealous about the other women, and then relieved because I said he never got serious. Well, just be careful with him. I don't want to see you hurt. If he asks you out, pray about it before you say yes. Please. As a favor to me."

"Oh, Clem. You're over-reacting."

"I don't think I am. Please, just promise me that you'll pray about it."

Dorrie smiled; she had already prayed about Liam enough that she could truthfully answer, "I promise. But you shouldn't be such a worry wart, you know, Clem. God will take care of me."

Clem looked at her friend and shook her head. "You're always so trusting. And I'm always so cautious, aren't I? What a combination we make." She went into her bedroom. "I don't know about you, but I'm exhausted from all this settling in. We'll talk more tomorrow, okay? Good night, Dorrie. Don't be mad at me about Liam. You know I love you."

Dorrie sighed and went into her own bedroom. She slid sweaters into drawers, hung dresses in the closet, and made up the bed with sheets and blankets. When she was done, she knew she was still filled with too much excited energy to be able to sleep. At college, Clem had always been the one in bed by ten, while Dorrie had stayed up late to study or talk with other friends.

Now, the quiet of the little house settled around her, but she was still buzzing with restlessness. She sat for a moment on her bed and tried to pray; around her, the house was absolutely still, a quietness that seemed to be waiting patiently, unchanging in its stillness. She shook her head at her imagination and jumped up to stare out her bedroom window at the moonlit field behind the house. A line of trees edged the back of the field, and behind them, Clem had told her, a river ran. On impulse, Dorrie pulled on her sneakers and slipped out the back door to go exploring.

Though the day had been warm, the cool night air against her face told her summer was nearly over. She pushed her way through the tall grass, soaking her jeans with dew. The tang of goldenrod filled the air and overhead wheeled the silent stars. She tipped her head back to see them. "Alleluia, alleluia," she whispered, then ran as hard and fast as she could to the edge of the field.

On the bank above the river she found a fallen log for a seat and settled herself there above the moonlit water's gleam and ripple. She took a deep breath, trying to relax her muscles and calm her heart.

Instead, she found herself breathing even faster, her arms hugged tight around her knees, while she remembered again every word Liam had spoken, every expression on his face, every look that had passed between them.

She had loved him so long. Back when she and Clem were both freshmen in college, he had seemed so much older, so far beyond her reach, but now the age difference was no longer as important. And Clem was right—something *had* been different tonight, something in the way he had smiled and said her name, the way he had listened when she'd talked, the way he had looked so deeply into her eyes.

Despite Clem's doubts, she had believed for a long time that Liam was the only man she could marry. That belief had kept her from getting serious with any of the other men she had dated, and whenever she had felt discouraged or lonely, she had told herself that in time, God would work things out. She hugged her knees tighter. This could finally be the time. Maybe God knew she and Liam were ready at last. When she had gotten the job at the children's home and known she would be working with Liam, she had been sure that her dreams would soon come true. God's hand was working; she knew it was.

She leaned back on the log and took another deep breath. Here outside, the night was quiet, just as it had been inside the house, but it was a busy sort of stillness, filled with the chirp of crickets, the gurgle of the river, and the sigh and flutter of the wind in the leaves. "Alleluia," she sang out loud, joining her voice with all the other night voices.

"Alleluia," a strange male voice answered her.

two

Dorrie froze. "Who's there?"

A dark shape rose from the edge of the river below her, a very large dark shape. She shrank back against her log as the man scrambled up the bank. "Alec MacIntyre," he said and held out his hand. "At your service."

Dorrie looked up into his face. In the moonlight, she could see only the slant of dark eyes above high square cheekbones. Her own face burned; she had thought she was all alone with God, and instead this stranger had been watching and listening. Reluctantly, she took his hand, then jerked away in surprise when he pulled her to her feet.

"Sorry," he said. "I just thought we might be able to see each other better if we were on the same level." But his head was still higher than hers, Dorrie realized. As tall as she was, she wasn't used to tipping her head back to see into someone's face; most of the men she knew were only a few inches taller than she was, but this man towered above her. She took a step backward.

"You must be my new neighbor," he said. "Clem told me you were coming today. My house is further down the road from yours and Clem's. I'm sorry I startled you. I heard you come, but I didn't want to disturb your solitude. Then when you sang, it echoed my own feelings so well—it's a beautiful night, isn't it?" When she didn't answer, he stepped closer to her and peered into her face. "You are Dorrie, aren't you?"

"Yes." He was so close she could feel his breath on her face. Dorrie took another step backward. "I really have to be getting back, Mr. MacIntyre."

She saw the gleam of his teeth and knew he smiled. He backed away from her and held up his hands. "I've scared you, haven't I? Sorry. My mother always says I'm like a St. Bernard dog, bumbling around, too stupid to know I'm scaring people with my size. I'm safe, honest. What do you think of your new house?"

"It's very nice." She would have liked to say, *You remind me more of some big buzzing insect, flitting from thing to thing, the way you talk*, but she pressed her lips together to keep back the words.

"I live in its twin—except I finally painted mine this summer. You and Clem will have to come over for supper one night. You can meet Esther."

"Your wife?"

He laughed. "My cat. I'm not married."

Dorrie could think of no response, and after a moment the silence made her shift her feet uncomfortably. She glanced up at his face and saw he was looking over her head across the moonlit river. "See the way the moon reflects in the river?" he said. "Like a million tiny lines of light. On nights like this, I can finally start to be quiet."

Not so I've noticed, Dorrie thought. He glanced at her as though he'd heard her thoughts and grinned. "I like to talk. You can probably tell that about me already. The trouble is, I like to think, too, so even when no one is around, all those words just keep pouring out of me. Sometimes I call it prayer—sometimes it *is* prayer—but sometimes all the noise I make keeps me from hearing God's voice. On a night like this, everything's so quiet, I get caught up in the beauty until I forget to make words inside my head. And in the midst of all the stillness and beauty, sometimes God's voice slips through. You know what I mean?"

"I'm not sure." For an instant she felt a flicker of understanding, but then he took another step closer to her. *I wish you would stop looming over me*, she thought. "I've had a long day, Mr. MacIntyre," she said out loud. "It was nice meeting you, but I've really got to get back now. I'm sure we'll run into each other again."

"Oh, we will." She saw his teeth flash again in the moonlight. "You see I teach at the children's home too. The grade below yours. Your room will be right down the hall from mine."

❧

"Alec is really very nice," Clem told her the next morning. She set down her coffee cup and giggled. "Although I can see how he must have startled you, rising out of the river bank like that. That's no reason to dislike the poor man, though."

Dorrie took a bite of toast. "I suppose. Something about him set my teeth on edge. He was just so—I don't know—big."

Clem giggled again. "That's certainly a good reason not to like him, Dorrie. How Christian of you."

"Well, he talked a lot, too. As though we'd been friends forever." She laughed sheepishly. "All right. I guess I was just embarrassed. I'll try to keep an open mind the next time I see—"

A loud honk interrupted her. Clem took her coffee cup to the front door and looked out. "I can't believe it. I've seen my brother more in the last two days than I usually do in two months." She turned to look at Dorrie with her eyebrows raised, but Dorrie had already leapt up and dashed to the bathroom mirror. She wiped toast crumbs from her mouth, ran a brush through her long hair, still damp from her morning's shower, and frowned at her blue jeans and old T-shirt.

"You're fine." Clem's voice was dry. "Go see what he wants."

Dorrie touched her wet hair. "Couldn't you talk to him while I blow-dry my hair? He's probably here to see you anyway—"

Clem waved an impatient hand. "I doubt it, Dorrie. Go on. I'll try to mind my own business."

Dorrie hesitated in the open door. Overhead, the sun gleamed through the oak leaves, casting a flickering pattern of light and shadow across Liam's face as he leaned out the window of his truck. He smiled. She looked back over her shoulder at Clem, then pulled the door shut behind her. "Hi," she said.

"Hi. I'm on my way to school to check over some new equipment. I thought maybe you'd like to come along. Look over your classroom. Get a feel for the place. I probably should have called, but I just thought of you when I drove by your road. Somehow I couldn't go past without at least stopping to say hello. I won't be offended if you have other plans for your day."

"No." Dorrie shoved her hands in her jeans' pockets to hide their trembling. "No, I'd—" She swallowed hard. "I'd love to go with you." She glanced down at her T-shirt. "Maybe you could give me a minute to change my clothes?

I don't think I look very professional."

Liam grinned and shook his head. "You don't look any less professional than I do. See?" He opened the truck door to show her his own jeans and T-shirt. "We won't be seeing any kids. And any other teachers who might come in today will be dressed just as casually. I've even seen Margaret Truesdell—that's our principal, you remember—in jeans during the break between semesters."

Dorrie remembered the dignified gray-haired woman and smiled. Her smile grew into laughter from sheer happiness. "Just let me tell Clem where I'm going."

In the truck, she sat on her hands so he wouldn't see the way she shook. She looked out the window and took long, deep breaths to calm herself.

He chuckled. "You look like an eager little kid, Dorrie. Sometimes I have to remind myself that you and Clem are really all grown up now." She glanced at him, and his smile widened. "And quite nicely, I might add. But I can't help but still feel protective. I hope this job doesn't prove to be a disappointment for you."

She kept her eyes on his face. "Why should it? I love working with kids. Being able to do it in a Christian setting sounds perfect."

Liam frowned, his eyes on the road. "These kids are a challenge, Dorrie," he said after a moment. "I don't want to mislead you. I know you'll be wonderful at the job, and I'm more glad than I can say to have you teaching here."

He pulled into the Home's long driveway. At the top of the hill, the brick school sprawled on one side of the road, while on the other a row of white cottages curved down into the woods. A group of children were playing on a playground, and Dorrie caught the shouts of a game being played on the soccer field beside them. Liam parked the car and stared at the boys running back and forth on the grass. He sighed.

"Next week it will be me out there with those boys, blowing my whistle, trying to teach them—" He shook his head. "Sorry, Dorrie. I always dread the end of my vacation. But I don't want to put a wet blanket on your enthusiasm."

Dorrie frowned. "But you do like your job, don't you, Liam? I always imagined it being the perfect spot for you—a place where you'd have room for both your love of God and your love of sports."

She couldn't decide the meaning of the twist he gave his mouth. He didn't say anything for a moment, just sat very still, while she searched his face with her eyes. "Just don't expect them to be loveable little tykes, Dorrie," he said at last. "Teaching them is a continual power struggle. I get tired of it sometimes." He took a breath and unlatched his door. "Come on. Enough sitting here while I brood. I know Margaret must have taken you on the official tour when she interviewed you, but let me show you around again. Then I'll leave you at your room while I go to the gym."

The building was empty except for a secretary typing in the main office. "Most of the teachers will be in later this week to get their rooms ready," Liam said. "Right now they're still vacationing. The break between the summer term and the fall semester is all too short."

Dorrie followed him down the shadowy halls, trying to memorize the location of library and faculty lounge, science lab and bathrooms. "What do the kids do while school's not in session?"

"The houseparents organize activities for them," Liam answered. "About two thirds of the kids go home, though, during break. Depending on the kid and what the situation is like at home." He pushed open a door at the end of the hall. "Here it is, the sixth grade classroom—your room. And here's your class list, already tacked to your bulletin board."

He handed Dorrie the sheet of paper. She glanced at it, then looked around the room. Twelve desks stood in a circle and bright checked curtains fluttered at the open window. Bookcases sectioned off a corner of the room where bean bag chairs were clustered on a bright rag rug. "I love it. Especially that reading corner."

Liam laughed. "That's one of Margaret's new ideas— but good luck getting the little monsters to sit still long enough to read. They're more likely to use the chairs as tumbling equipment—or the books as missiles. These kids aren't exactly the bookish sort."

Dorrie looked at him. "You're so negative today."

"Not negative. Just honest." His hand touched her cheek. Dorrie froze, forgetting everything but the feel of his fingers against her skin. "I hope you're happy in this classroom, Dorrie." His voice was soft. "I hope the job's everything you want it to be."

He was standing so close to her that she was certain she could feel his warmth, like a blanket she longed to pull around her shoulders. Her breath came faster and faster, and then his hand dropped from her face. He moved away. "I'd rather stay here with you, believe me, but if I can get my work done now, maybe we could go out for lunch?"

"I'd like that," she managed to say.

"Then I'll see you in an hour or two."

After he had left the room, she sank down into one of the bean bag chairs, replaying their conversation in her mind. She put her hand to her face where his fingers had touched her.

At last, she remembered the class list in her hand and looked down at it. Eight boys and four girls. She read their names over, imagining their faces, then found her way back to the main office to ask the secretary for their records.

While she was waiting for Mrs. Hutter to pull the folders from the filing cabinet, the door opened behind her. "Why, hello, Dorrie."

Dorrie turned around. "Hello, Mrs. Truesdell." She smiled at the principal, noticing that as Liam had predicted, she was dressed in jeans and a cotton shirt. "I'm about to start getting to know my new students."

Margaret Truesdell smiled. "They're some of my favorite kids." She waited while Dorrie collected the pile of folders and thanked Mrs. Hutter. "I'll walk with you up to your classroom."

They climbed the stairs in silence. Dorrie noticed that the top of Margaret's silver head came only to her shoulder, but the older woman carried herself with such an air of assurance and authority that Dorrie found herself feeling very young beside her.

They reached Dorrie's classroom, and Dorrie dropped the folders on her desk. Margaret walked around the room. "What do you think? Have you noticed anything missing, anything you think you'll need?"

Dorrie shook her head. "Not yet. I really just got here. Liam Adams drove me over." She felt her cheeks grow warm, as though Margaret's cool gray eyes could somehow read that she'd spent her time so far dreaming about Liam. "I haven't had a chance to really look things over yet," she finished, trying to sound composed and professional.

Margaret nodded. She straightened one of the bean bag chairs, then looked over her shoulder at Dorrie. "Did Liam tell you what he thinks of my reading nooks, my newest additions to the rooms?"

Dorrie hesitated. "He was a little pessimistic."

Margaret nodded. "To say the least, I'm sure. I hope you won't let his attitude influence you too much."

"Oh, I think a reading corner is a wonderful idea," Dorrie answered. "If I were a child, I would love to curl up here and read."

Margaret shook her head. "These children won't. Not at first. Liam's absolutely right—they have no idea of the proper use for chairs and books. But my philosophy is, they will never learn different ways if they're not given the opportunity. When I was growing up, reading was the way I escaped, the thing that kept me sane—and one of the main ways that God touched me during those years. Most of these children will eventually have to go back to lives that are far from perfect. Unfortunately, there's nothing we can do to change those lives very much. But we can help them to grow strong—and offer them some escape hatches. Like books. Something besides drugs and sex, the only escapes they usually can find on their own."

Margaret ran her hand through her short gray hair, then turned toward the window. She was silent for a moment. Dorrie looked at the delicate, narrow bones of her face and waited. "Liam may have told you," Margaret said at last, her eyes still focused on the playing field outside the window, "these aren't easy children. They don't open their hearts easily—and because of that you may find it more difficult to open your heart to them." Dorrie made a movement, as though to deny Margaret's words; the older woman glanced at her and smiled. "That may not be the case with you. I remember very clearly your recommendation from your internship supervisor—she said you have a loving heart for wounded children. That's one of the main reasons I hired you. But loving hearts are sometimes easily hurt, and these children are experts at hurting others. They've learned to be that way to protect themselves."

Margaret sighed. She put her hand on Dorrie's arm and looked up into her face. "I'd like to suggest, Dorrie, that you go slowly with these kids. Be patient with them. Be patient with yourself. Keep your heart quiet. Pay close attention to who these children really are, and how it is that God wants to speak to them. Try to let God use you in whatever way He wants. This isn't the sort of job you can come to with your mind on other things. It needs your whole attention."

Her lips curved a little, and she shook her head. "I probably don't make any sense to you right now, do I? You'll have to wait till you've been with the kids for a while. September is always such a hectic month—if I forget to schedule an appointment with you, track me down and make sure we talk again." Her smile widened. "I'm glad you're here, Dorrie."

After she had gone, Dorrie turned to the stack of folders. For the first time since she had been hired for this job, she found herself forgetting about Liam and what working with him could mean for their relationship. Instead, Margaret had helped her to realize the reality of the children she would soon be teaching. "After all, God, I must be here for them too, not just because of Liam," she said. She worked her way through the twelve folders, filling several sheets of paper with notes and ideas.

The room was very quiet, but she barely noticed. Only once, she heard a small rustle from somewhere in the room. She looked up from her paper; *a mouse*, she thought, and imagined a small, bright-eyed creature sharing the quiet with her. "I don't know how you can stand those little things," her mother would always say and shudder, but Dorrie liked mice. She smiled and picked up her pen once more.

At last, she stood up and stretched, then went to the shelves that lined one wall to inspect the supplies and text-books. She leaned back against the shelves and looked around the room, noticing for the first time how still it was.

The sun poured through the windows, laying squares of light across the desks and wooden floor. Faintly, she could hear the shouts from the soccer game, but that was the only noise. For once, she felt comfortable with the quiet, as though something in the room's calm had washed over her busy heart, leaving her cleaner and more peaceful than before.

"I know You're here, God," she said softly. "I can almost feel Your Spirit's breath. Please use me in this room. Let the children see You through me. Help them to learn and grow strong and whole."

She leaned forward and opened a closet door, expecting to find more supplies. Instead, her eyes fell on a nearly life-size drawing of a tiger. A small sound made her eyes drop lower. She froze.

She caught the gleam of glasses. From behind them, a pair of brown and unfriendly eyes stared back at her.

three

"You're not a mouse."

The boy's mouth twisted. "Of course not. That time I made that rustling noise, it was because I had to scratch my arm. That was the only time I moved at all, but I figured you heard me. I can sit still for hours usually, but the mosquitoes were wicked last night. We had evening devotions outside. What a stupid idea. If I hadn't been covered with bites, I never would have moved at all. You thought I was a mouse? Bet you were scared, weren't you? Did you jump up on top of your desk?"

Dorrie shook her head. "I like mice. Although I suppose I wouldn't want to share my house with them if I could help it."

"Ephesians Cottage had mice this summer. They poisoned them. Do you like my tiger?"

Dorrie looked again at the drawing. "He's beautiful. Where did you get him?"

"I drew him, stupid. I'm pretty good, aren't I? Isn't he awesome?"

"Totally." She smiled at him, but his eyes flicked away from her gaze. "I'm impressed. You're very talented."

He shrugged. "I'm also very intelligent. I'm the smartest kid at the Home. I'm probably smarter than you are. My IQ is 148. So I really don't need a teacher, at least not one like you. It's irrational to make me go to school here."

"So why do you think you're here?"

29

He shrugged and made a face. "My mom kept locking me out of the trailer. I drive her crazy. She used to hit me with her hairbrush till I'd run outside, and then she'd lock the door quick. I got so, though, I'd go outside as soon as she picked up the brush. It was no big deal really. There was a hole underneath the trailer I could crawl into. I used to keep things there, kind of like this closet. But then last winter, one of our nosy neighbors called child protective. A couple of other things happened at school, too."

"Like what?"

He shrugged again. "Oh, this jerk tried to shove me around." He stared up into Dorrie's face. "He was the gym teacher," he said significantly, "just like Mr. Adams. Anyways, I lost my cool. They say I hit him and yelled all sorts of stuff. He shouldn't have touched me, though. They said I was emotionally disturbed. Eventually, I ended up here. I hate this place."

He was still sitting hunched in the dark closet. She could see very little of him except the straight dark hair that fell across his glasses. "Who are you anyway?" she asked.

"Felix."

She picked up her class list and looked down at it. "Felix Jones. Right? I'm Miss Carpenter. You're going to be in my class next week when classes start. What are you doing in my closet?"

"It's not *your* closet."

"All right." She smiled. "What are you doing in *the* closet?"

"What's it look like I'm doing?"

She shrugged. "I don't know. You can't have been doing much of anything. With the door closed, it must be pitch black in here."

"There's a light, stupid. I turned it off when I heard you walking this way. I was hoping you wouldn't see me. People usually only see what they're expecting to see."

"It was kind of hard to miss that tiger," Dorrie said mildly. She noticed then the long string hanging from the bulb in the ceiling and reached out to pull it. With its light, she could see that the walk-in closet was filled with neatly stacked drawing paper, books, boxes of colored pencils, pastels, and markers, and watercolor paints. A row of apples was lined up along one shelf, and drawings of animals were taped everywhere. Felix sat on a bean bag chair, his finger in a book. His knees were hunched close to his small shoulders, and his brown eyes glared up at Dorrie.

"I'm small for my age."

Dorrie nodded.

"But I'm smarter than you."

"I remember you mentioned that."

"I'm probably even smarter than—" He broke off, and his gaze shifted beyond Dorrie's face. She saw his face grow tighter. "I'm definitely smarter than *him*," he finished.

Dorrie turned to find Liam standing behind her. "Look who I found." She moved to let Liam see into the closet.

Liam frowned. "Just what do you think you're doing here, Mr. Jones? Where are you supposed to be?"

Felix got to his feet, his shoulders straight and tense. "I'm *supposed* to be playing some idiotic game, *Mr.* Adams. You'll remember, though, that I don't like games."

Liam shook his head. "I suggest, Mr. Jones, you get back to wherever it is you belong. You know the school building is off limits when classes aren't in session. I'll speak to your houseparents to make sure you get the proper number of demerits. Which cottage are you in?"

"Why should I tell you?"

Dorrie had never seen Liam's face look so hard. "Because if you waste my time by making me look it up, I'll see that you get double the usual amount of demerits. You won't have to worry about playing stupid games, because you won't be seeing anything except the inside of the detention center."

Felix shrugged. "I like detention. I know someone with your limited mental abilities, Mr. Adams, wouldn't understand—but I like to have uninterrupted time to think. No one bothers me in detention. But if it will make you happier—I live in Corinthians."

Dorrie stepped forward to end the confrontation. "I'll look forward to seeing you next week, Felix."

Felix ducked past her. "Wait just a minute, Mr. Jones," snapped Liam. "You owe me an apology for your rudeness, don't you think?" Before Felix could respond, Liam stepped forward and grabbed a corner of the tiger drawing. "And get your things out of Miss Carpenter's closet."

Dorrie put her hand on Liam's arm. "No, I—"

Before she could say more, Felix sprang between Liam and the drawing, his small face screwed tight. "Don't you touch that!" He knocked Liam's hand away from the drawing.

"Now, see here—"

Dorrie felt the muscles in Liam's arms clench, and she clutched him tighter. "No, Liam," she whispered. "Let it go."

He glanced at her, then shrugged his arm free. "You're coming with me, Mr. Jones. Straight to the detention center."

Felix stood small and straight, his back pressed against his drawing. "I'm not going anywhere. You can't make me." His voice wavered, but his chin came up and his eyes locked with Liam's.

Dorrie tried to think of a way to end the power struggle, a way that would save face for both Liam and Felix, but her mind was blank.

"Hi, everybody," said a calm voice.

A man leaned against the door frame of her classroom. From his size, she knew who he had to be. She watched Alec MacIntyre's dark eyes move from face to face. "Looks like your hideout was discovered, Felix." He smiled at Dorrie. "I hope you don't mind that I gave Felix permission to use this closet for his things. Privacy's a pretty slim commodity around here."

"You gave him permission?" Liam looked as though he didn't believe it.

Alec nodded. "So long as he checks in with his houseparents whenever he comes here. He needed a safe place for his books and art work."

Liam turned back to Felix. "Why didn't you say so?"

"You didn't ask."

Dorrie heard Liam take a deep breath.

"Sometimes a simple explanation saves everyone a lot of trouble, Felix," Alec said easily. "Come on, why don't we show Miss Carpenter the wall mural you did in my room last year."

Felix's shoulders relaxed. He stepped away from the

tiger drawing, then glanced from Liam to Dorrie.

"You're welcome to this space, Felix," Dorrie said. "But maybe we could hang the tiger on the outside of the door instead of inside. That way everybody could appreciate it. If you don't mind."

"No." Felix shook his head and closed the closet door firmly behind him. "The other kids would ruin it." He followed Alec to the door.

"Mr. MacIntyre?" Liam said. Alec looked back over his shoulder. "I'm not very happy with this situation you've set up. Could we talk about it another time?"

Alec shrugged. "At your convenience." His eyes moved to Dorrie. "Coming?"

"Miss Carpenter and I are going out to lunch," Liam said stiffly. "Another time, Mr. MacIntyre."

Dorrie looked from Alec to Liam. She had known last night in the dark that Alec was several inches taller than Liam, but she had not realized how much bigger he was all over. Next to Alec's broad shoulders and lanky arms and legs, Liam's slim frame looked trim and neat. Alec's brown hair curled wildly above the square, prominent bones of his face, while Liam's black head was smooth and narrow. *Like the difference between a well-groomed thoroughbred and some huge farm horse,* Dorrie thought to herself. She saw that Liam's expression was as stiff as his voice had been, and when she turned back to Alec, she hated the small smile on his lips, as though he knew he had been able to handle a situation that had been too much for Liam. She wanted to turn away from Alec MacIntyre, she wanted to go out to lunch with Liam and forget all about him. But something about the set of Felix's small shoulders changed her mind.

"Could you wait just a few minutes?" she asked Liam. "I would like to see Felix's mural."

"Whatever. I'll be in the truck."

Dorrie watched him stride across the room and out the door, hoping his anger would not destroy the new warmth that had been growing between them. She turned to find Alec's eyes on her face.

"We won't take long," he said quietly. "I don't want to interfere with your lunch date."

Felix looked up at her as they walked down the hall to the fifth grade classroom. "You're going out with Mr. *Adams*?"

Dorrie's cheeks grew warm. "We're just having lunch together. He gave me a ride here today."

"Do you *like* him?"

"Yes, I do."

Felix shrugged. "What can you expect from someone who talks to herself? Your perception of reality is obviously severely distorted."

"What do you mean?" Dorrie smiled.

"I heard you. When I was in the closet. First, you were talking to Mr. Adams. 'Believe me, Dorrie, I'd rather stay here with you.' It made me want to gag. And then after a while you and Mrs. Truesdell talked. And then I'm sure you were all alone. And I heard you talking."

"Oh." Dorrie laughed. "I think I was talking to God."

Felix's mouth twisted. "Aren't you too old for an imaginary friend? Now, I know you're crazy, talking to someone no one's ever seen."

Alec put his hand on Felix's shoulder. "Look at this," he

said to Dorrie, pointing to a mural of the solar system on his classroom wall. "Didn't Felix do a great job? Didn't you tell me, Felix, you used some of Copernicus' drawings when you were doing this?"

"That's right."

"Funny, isn't it, that Copernicus could portray some of the outermost planets when he had never seen them?"

"He could tell they were there by their effect on the planets he could see," Felix said. "Their gravitational pull."

"Maybe one way we can see God is by the way He affects the world around us."

Felix shook his head. "I knew you were working up to one of your bad analogies. Copernicus never *talked* to those planets. The fact that something *may* exist doesn't imply we should pretend to have a personal relationship with it."

"Well, I guess you're right about the analogy not being a very good one. Maybe Miss Carpenter talks to God, though, because the effects of His love in her life are more evident and constant than the gravitational pull of a distant planet."

Felix scowled. "He hasn't been real *or* constant in *my* life."

"You'd be surprised." Alec's voice was gentle. He glanced up at the clock. "Go on with you now, or you'll be late for lunch. I'll see you next week."

After Felix was gone, Alec turned to Dorrie. "He's an interesting kid. And very bright."

"He told me."

Alec laughed. "He would. He's also very wounded. Like most of the kids here. It's hard to believe in God's love when you have doubts about your own mother's love."

Dorrie nodded. She looked at Alec's strong features,

surprised by the gentleness she saw there.

"You were good with him," he said, his eyes on her face.

Dorrie looked away. *Thank you for granting me your approval*, she wanted to say, but instead she shrugged. "I like him."

"I'm sorry about the situation that developed over the closet. I got Margaret's approval, but I should have put a memo in all the faculty's boxes. My own closet is chock full, and I thought I'd have a chance to talk to you about it before you came into school. I never would have set Felix up for a run-in with Liam Adams. If I had thought things through better, I should have realized you and he would be friends, and Liam would be apt to come to your room before classes started. Liam and Felix haven't gotten along since the day Felix got here."

"Felix told me he had a problem with a gym teacher in his old school. Maybe that's why his attitude is bad about Liam."

Alec shrugged. "Maybe."

They were silent for a moment. Again Dorrie was aware of how quiet the school building was, but this time she longed to escape from the silence. She looked past Alec and through the window saw Liam sitting in his truck, his arm resting on the open window while his fingers drummed on the roof top. Alec turned to follow her gaze. "I've held you up, haven't I?" he said. "I'm sorry."

"That's okay." She took a step toward the doorway, longing to hurry outside to Liam, but Alec put his hand on her arm. She looked down at his large fingers, and something like a shudder ran through her body.

"At the risk of sounding as though I have the social skills

of Felix Jones," he said, his brown eyes smiling into hers, "I'd like to ask you something."

Dorrie was nearly jiggling with impatience, longing to be gone. "Yes?"

"*Are* you and Liam dating?"

"No." *But I'd like to be*, her heart cried.

"Then would you go to dinner with me tonight?"

four

"I would never have thought he'd ask me out," Dorrie said to Clem later that afternoon. They sat on their front lawn, fishing leaves out of the blackberries they had just picked.

Clem grinned. "I was hoping you and Alec would hit it off. When is he picking you up?"

"He's not. And we're not. He makes me uncomfortable. Your Gram would probably tell me to pray about my attitude—but I really don't like him very much. So I told him I wanted to spend the evening with you. It's true. I feel like I've hardly seen you yet."

Clem set aside her berry basket. "Well, you're not going to see me tonight. Mason called me at work today. He asked if we could get together tonight. He says he needs to talk to me about something." She leaned back on her hands and frowned. "I'm sorry, Dorrie."

Dorrie popped a berry into her mouth. "That's all right. We'll have lots of time together. Mainly, I just wanted an excuse for not going out with Alec."

"But why? Why don't you like him?"

Dorrie shrugged. "I don't know." She tipped back her head to watch the flicker of oak leaves overhead. "Something about him just rubs me the wrong way. He seems so—I don't know. Smug. Like he knows all the answers."

"I don't think he's like that really. He just likes to talk. You'd like him if you got to know him, I know you would. The two of you have a lot in common, I've thought so ever since I met him."

Dorrie looked at her friend. "Don't you go matchmaking, Clementine Adams. I'm truly not interested. Not in the least."

Clem held up her hands and laughed. "I won't. Promise. But I guess I did hope that—"

"What?"

"Oh, that when you saw Alec and Liam together, you'd see how much more—real, I guess, Alec is than Liam."

Dorrie snorted. "Will you stop that, Clem? Why are you so negative about your own brother? As a matter of fact, when I saw them together, I had the opposite reaction—I thought Liam was the much more attractive of the two. Alec looks like a huge clodhopper next to Liam."

Clem's delicate eyebrows pulled together. "Alec's attractive, Dorrie. But I wasn't referring to their looks. Alec is always honest and open, whereas Liam—" She threw up her hands. "You know what I think. Just look at the difference in the way the two of them handled that boy in your closet. Liam was angry and rigid, heading for a confrontation—"

"I never said he was perfect," Dorrie interrupted. "So he's having some problems with his job—that doesn't mean I'll stop caring for him. And remember how you were complaining that Liam seems too perfect, that he never shares his problems? Well, today he was sharing with me his feelings about his job. I think he's feeling a little burnt out. At lunch, he even asked me to pray for him. This job is so right for him—I know God will show him the way to get back his enthusiasm."

"I'm glad he talked to you like that." Clem smiled at Dorrie, but the two small lines between her brows told

Dorrie she was still worried. Clem picked a small green worm off a berry and set it carefully on a blade of grass. "I never did think Liam was particularly well-suited for working with kids."

Dorrie sighed. "Will you listen to yourself? You can't say anything good about Liam."

Clem looked up from the worm, her blue eyes round and wide. "It's no sin to be poorly suited for working with kids. Some people are, some people aren't. You and Mason and Alec happen to be very good at it. I'm not. I don't think Liam is either. That has nothing to do with my other worries about him. Except that I wonder if you even see the real Liam. I worry that you've fallen in love with a fantasy—your idea of who Liam is instead of who he really is."

Dorrie grabbed her berry basket and got to her feet. "You're wrong, Clem." The screen door slapped shut behind her.

She poured the berries into a colander and rinsed them under the faucet. "Shall I make these into a pie?" she asked when Clem had followed her inside.

"That would be wonderful." Clem handed her the other berry basket. She leaned against the counter beside Dorrie. "I'm sorry," she said after a moment. "I keep telling myself to mind my own business about you and Liam. My only excuse this time is that I'm nervous."

Dorrie looked up from the berries. "About what?"

"I'm scared of what Mason wants to say to me tonight. He sounded so serious."

Dorrie dumped the berries into a bowl. She smiled. "Maybe he has something important he wants to ask you."

Clem shook her head. "I don't think so."

Dorrie laughed. "You are such a pessimist, Clemmie. A regular little Eeyore. Now go on." She gave Clem's arm a push. "Your hands are all scratched and stained, your lips are purple from sneaking berries when you thought I wasn't looking, and your hair is full of twigs. Go take a shower and make yourself beautiful. I have a feeling that tonight's the night Mason will finally get up his nerve. You worry too much. This world is run by a God who loves us, remember?"

"That doesn't mean He gives us nothing but happy endings, though," Clem muttered, but she disappeared into the bathroom and turned on the shower.

❧

Dorrie set the blackberry pie on the counter to cool. With Clem out with Mason, the house was quiet. Once again, the stillness irritated Dorrie. It seemed almost like a hand patiently stretched out, waiting to be held. She shook her head at her fancies and moved restlessly from the living room to her bedroom, then back to the kitchen. She got herself a glass of water, looked in the refrigerator, turned the radio on and then off again.

At last, she gathered up her textbooks and teaching ideas, and with her canvas bag full, she went outside and back through the field to the river. For several minutes, she worked furiously, but then her chin in her hand, her eyes on the river's ripple, her mind drifted away from curriculum planning. Instead, it circled around and around the thought of Liam.

"You and Clem tired of each other already?"

Dorrie jumped. Alec MacIntyre was stretched out by the river just below her, his brown corduroy pants and dark green T-shirt blending with the leaves and bark around him. "You again!" She flushed. "Mason wanted to see Clem," she said guiltily.

He lay on his back looking up at her for a moment, perfectly still, his dark eyes watching her, and then he sat up. "You could have called me. Or we could still go get something to eat together. It's not too late, and I for one haven't eaten yet. What about you?"

He climbed up beside her, moving aside an arithmetic book so that he could settle next to her on the fallen log. She wanted to inch further away from him, but she could feel his eyes on her. She kept her own gaze fixed on the river. "I'm not particularly hungry," she said. Immediately, her stomach growled loudly, and her cheeks burned.

He smiled, and then said softly, "Something tells me you're not particularly interested in seeing any more of me than you have to."

She couldn't think of an answer. *You don't believe in beating around the bush, do you?* she thought; *if you get the message, then why can't you politely go away?* She felt guilty for her thoughts, but before she could form a courteous response to his words, he said gently, "That's all right. Although I wasn't asking for a lifetime commitment. Just an evening out. A chance to get to know each other better. I guess I've been feeling lonely lately, and when I met you, I thought—" He shrugged his shoulders.

She made herself turn and meet his eyes. "I'm sorry. Maybe it's just that you seem to keep popping up when I'm least prepared." She tried to smile. "Like a jack-in-the-box. At least this time you didn't catch me singing."

His mouth softened. His eyes rested on the river; she glanced down at his large hands lying quietly on his knees, and she thought of the way Liam's hands constantly moved.

Liam seemed always driven by a restless energy; she knew he would never be able to sit here like Alec, absolutely still.

"Sometimes," Alec said, his eyes still on the river, "I think God likes to surprise us so that He can show us Himself. We like to figure things out and put God all neat and tidy in a box. Then we can get busy with our lives and forget to pay daily attention to Who our God really is. I do it all the time—but then He shows me He's bigger than any box I could ever imagine. He surprises me. Like a jack-in-the-box. That's why I love the unexpected. Like finding you here last night, and then again today. If my heart is quiet enough, if I'm not too busy to even notice, sometimes I catch a brand new glimpse of God's face."

Dorrie frowned. "I'm not sure I know what you mean."

Alec smiled. "You have the most beautiful hair, did you know? When the sun shines on it, it looks just like a flame."

Dorrie felt her face grow warm. She put her hand to her hair, as though to hide it, and looked away from his smiling eyes. *First you babble about God being a jack-in-the-box, and now you try to feed me a line about my hair,* she thought. *Why can't you just leave? Sitting here like this with you, you bother me. You're just too—big.*

"Sorry," he said. "Sometimes I have the bad habit of saying whatever pops into my head." She felt his eyes on her face, but when she finally took her own eyes from the river, he was looking down, studying an ant that was climbing his leg. "Sometimes," he said, "I probably talk too much all together."

Dorrie listened to the ripple of the water and the cawing of a crow. Somehow, the sounds seemed only to add to the quiet, the same way Alec's voice had blended with the stillness. She remembered the busy restaurant Liam had taken her to for lunch, the constant motion of his face and hands as he and she ate and talked, and she wished she could be there again with him, instead of here with Alec. She shifted uncomfortably on the log and searched for something to say. "What did you mean about God surprising us?" she asked at last.

She heard him sigh. "I guess I was thinking about Isaiah 55 where God says, 'For my thoughts are not your thoughts, neither are your ways my ways.' In my mind, I always put that together with what it says in Psalm 46, 'Be still, and know that I am God.' Sometimes I get so impressed with my own ideas that I miss what God really wants for me. My head's too full with my own noisy thinking to catch that 'still small voice.'" He turned his head and his dark eyes studied her face. "I'm afraid that's what I've been doing with you."

She pulled a blade of grass and began tearing it into tiny pieces. "What do you mean?"

He smiled. "I mean I think you're awfully pretty, Dorrie Carpenter. In fact, I've been thinking of very little else all day long. And now I can see it's time to quiet down my heart so that I can hear God's voice again. Sometimes His surprises don't mean exactly what we'd like them to." He got to his feet. "I'm sorry I intruded on your privacy yet another time." He looked down at her and one corner of his wide mouth turned up. "I guess I'll have to find myself another hide-out. Otherwise, every time one of us wants to be alone by the river, we'll find ourselves bumping into each other instead." He touched one finger to the top of her head. "I'll see you later, Dorrie."

Dorrie watched him go, his long legs jumping easily over

rocks and fallen logs, until he had disappeared between the trees around the river's bend. She felt the warmth of the evening sun on the top of her head, the same place he'd touched her. She put up her hand as though she could rub the warmth away.

She spread out her work again and tried to concentrate. After a few minutes, she slapped her notebook shut and piled her books back in the bag. *I think you're awfully pretty, Dorrie Carpenter*, she heard his voice say inside her head, and she shook her head impatiently. She got to her feet and made her way back across the field to the house.

When she went in the back door, she was surprised to find Clem scrubbing furiously at the baking dishes Dorrie had left in the sink.

"You're home early," Dorrie said. "How come?"

Two tears dripped off Clem's cheeks into the dishwater. "I can't talk about it right now, Dorrie." Her voice was choked.

Dorrie looked at her bent head, then went to the front door and saw Mason still sitting in his car in the driveway. She looked back at Clem, then softly opened the door and went outside.

"What's going on?" she asked Mason through his open window.

He was slouched down behind the wheel; at her voice, he turned his head, and she barely recognized his face. Mason always smiled, she realized, but now his mouth turned down and his eyes were blank. He shrugged his shoulders. "I don't know, Dorrie. I don't understand her."

Dorrie made a face. "Come on, Mason. She's not that hard to understand. You two have been going together for years now. The whole world expects you to get married. You can't blame her for thinking about it, too. In fact, I don't think it makes much sense for your relationship to just go on and on like this, unless it's leading somewhere."

"I know." Mason stared straight ahead at the dashboard. "But every time I've tried to talk about the future, Clem's always changed the subject. It's like it scares her. I've applied to a mission board—and I need to tell them whether I'll be married or single. Tonight I had to find out where I stood."

"What are you talking about? Clem's in there crying."

"I know." Mason's voice was husky. "I don't understand what she wants. I asked her to marry me. But she said no."

five

"How could you tell him no?" Dorrie asked. "Here, you've been complaining to me about how Mason never wants to get serious. And now he tells me the same thing—about you! What is it with the two of you?"

Clem leaned her forehead against the kitchen wall. "I know, I know," she said, her voice muffled. "I must be losing my mind. I don't understand myself any better than you do." She raised her tear-streaked face and looked at Dorrie. "I thought I wanted to marry him more than anything else in the world. I really did. But when I heard him asking me, actually saying the words—I don't know. All I could feel was scared. Terrified. Like something wasn't right. I couldn't say yes."

Dorrie put her arm around Clem's shoulders. "But did you have to say no? Poor Mason. He was sitting out there in his car like a dog who had just been kicked. He had tears in his eyes."

Clem gulped back a sob. "I know, I know. That's why I feel so terrible. I know how much I've hurt him."

Dorrie looked at the fresh tears welling in Clem's eyes. "Don't you think it's like you said—you just got scared? It wouldn't hurt you so much to see Mason hurt if you didn't really love him."

"I *know* I love him." Clem pushed away from Dorrie. "That's not the problem. It just doesn't feel right." She grabbed a tissue and blew her nose. "I don't think it can be

God's will for us to be together after all."

"Oh, Clemmie. Are you sure?"

Clem sniffed. "I can't talk anymore, Dorrie. Crying always makes me sleepy. I've got to go to bed. Maybe things will make more sense tomorrow."

"I hope so. I'll be praying, Clem."

❧

But the next day and for the remainder of the week, Clem refused to talk about Mason. At church on Sunday, Dorrie saw Mason's gaze go again and again to Clem, but Clem kept her eyes fixed on her grandfather as he preached; her round face was calm and still, but the rosiness was gone from her cheeks.

Dorrie's own eyes were drawn to Liam's narrow, dark face. She watched the earnest way he turned the pages of his Bible, the way his attention never faltered from his grandfather's sermon, and she smiled to herself. *Oh, God*, she prayed silently, *I love him so much.*

Once as she looked across the church, her eye caught Alec MacIntyre's. He looked away quickly, and so did she.

When the last hymn had been sung and Grandpop Adams had pronounced the benediction, Dorrie tried to steer Clem in the direction of Liam and Mason as they stood talking in the vestibule. Clem, however, her small face set, grabbed Dorrie's elbow and pulled her in the opposite direction.

"Hello, Alec." Clem smiled. "I hear you and Dorrie keep stumbling over each other."

Alec put the pile of hymnals he carried in the corner of a pew. "Afraid so." He stretched for another hymnal, and did not look at the two girls.

Dorrie pulled surreptitiously at Clem's arm, but Clem ignored her. "You all ready for classes to start tomorrow?"

Clem took a step closer to Alec and smiled up at him. "Dorrie's been going into school every day to work in her room. I think she's starting to get a little obsessed. I swear I heard her muttering about bulletin boards in her sleep last night."

"Oh, you did not." Dorrie shook her head at Clem, trying to signal with her eyes her longing to be gone.

"Good morning, Clem, Dorrie." Dorrie turned with relief away from Alec to Clem's grandmother. "I've just invited the boys to dinner. We want you two girls, too, of course." The small, white-haired woman put out her hand and caught Alec's sleeve as he was turning away. "You, too, Alec. We've plenty of food."

Clem's smile had disappeared. "The boys, Gram?"

"Yes, of course, dear." Her grandmother's eyes had gone beyond Clem, and her voice was absent. "Liam and Mason."

"But, Gram, I can't—"

"Excuse me, dear, but I have to talk to Mrs. Simpson about the flowers for next week. I'll see you all in about a half hour at the house."

"But—" Clem turned helplessly to Dorrie. "I can't eat dinner with Mason. Not now."

Dorrie grinned. "Serves you right." She looked at Alec as he looked after Gram Adams, his dark eyes unreadable. Dorrie's smile faded, and she added softly, "Not that I'm any happier about this arrangement than you are."

Alec's eyes met hers. He shrugged. "I guess we will all go and have dinner. I think we were just issued our orders."

Dorrie nodded. "Gram Adams is a wonderful cook," she said politely. She looked across the church, and caught

Liam's blue gaze. Her smile returned. She could put up
with having dinner with Alec MacIntyre as long as Liam
would be there, too.

ک

Dorrie ate her last bite of apple pie and leaned back in her
chair. She looked around the Adams' dining room, from
the red geraniums on the windowsills to the baskets and
copper kettles that lined the shelves. The room, like the
rest of the house, was as cozy and welcoming as the
English cottages in the prints Gram had given Clem for
their new house. Dorrie looked from Grandpop Adams,
with his thin white hair and beaklike nose, to Gram, who
looked exactly the way Clem would look in another fifty
years, from her round, childlike face to her small, practi-
cal body. Dorrie smiled, glad that when she and Liam were
married, she would belong to Gram and Grandpop, too.

Gram had seated her between Liam and Alec, across
from Clem and Mason. Clem had kept her eyes on her
plate, never glancing at Mason once during the entire meal,
saying very little. Alec was as quiet as Clem, but Liam,
Dorrie, and Mason had discussed upcoming church
activities with Grandpop Adams. Mason's voice was
strained, though, and he kept glancing sideways at Clem,
trying to include her in the conversation. She seemed unaware of him, her blue eyes cloudy and preoccupied.

From her end of the table, Gram had been watching them
all quietly. "What did you think of the sermon today,
Dorrie?" she asked now, a hint of a smile in the round blue
eyes that were so much like Clem's.

"I—" Dorrie hesitated; she searched her memory, but
she could not call to mind even the text Grandpop had
used. "I always love Grandpop's sermons," she said at last.

"How tactful, dear," Gram murmured, the smile in her eyes growing. She turned to Clem. "What about you, Clem? Did you agree with Grandpop's interpretation of Paul's words?"

Clem's eyes rose from her plate to meet her grandmother's gaze, and her cheeks took on their usual rosiness. "I'll have to think about it."

"Ah." Gram's white head nodded. "How wise of you. Never a good idea to leap to an opinion rashly." Her eyes went next to Alec.

Dorrie saw that he was waiting for Gram's question, his dark eyes gleaming. "And you, Alec? Were you able to form an opinion about the sermon?"

He grinned. "I'm sorry, Mrs. Adams, but I have to be honest—I'm afraid my mind was on other things this morning."

Mason smiled shamefacedly. "Before it's my turn, I'll confess, too, Gram." He shrugged his shoulders and looked around the table. "What a sorry bunch we are. Is that why you insisted we all come to dinner—so you could show us how inattentive we were to God's Word?"

Gram shook her head reproachfully. "Of course not, Mason. That's between you and the Lord. I was just a little amused, watching the four of you. Your minds were so obviously on other things."

Her husband leaned back in his chair and laughed. "Well, at least you children will keep me humble. I looked out at your faces, and I felt proud knowing you were all listening to me so attentively." He reached for his coffee cup and laughed again.

"Poor Grandpop." Liam turned to his grandfather. "Casting your pearls before these swine. I for one can tell you exactly what I thought about your sermon." He grinned at Clem. "I certainly know your text had nothing to do with anything Paul wrote, since it was from the book of Isaiah."

Clem stuck out her tongue at Liam. She pushed back her chair and joined Alec as he collected dirty dishes from the table. "How about if Dorrie and Alec and I do these dishes as our penance?" she said. She gave her grandmother a gentle push. "You go sit in the living room and tell Mason what it was he missed at church today. The rest of us swine will clean up the mess in the kitchen."

Clem kept up a stream of chatter while Alec washed the dishes, and she and Dorrie dried. Alec and Dorrie worked silently, answering Clem when she asked a question but never looking at each other. From the corner of her eye, Dorrie was aware of Alec's white sleeves rolled up above his elbows and the dark hairs that grew down his arms and onto his long-fingered hands. Once when she reached for a dish from the hot rinse water, her hand brushed Alec's bare arm; they both pulled away as quickly as if they had been burned.

Clem fell quiet, and for several minutes they worked in silence. Through the door into the dining room, Dorrie could hear Liam and his grandfather discussing the morning's sermon. She listened to the rise and fall of Liam's tenor voice, and she smiled, but Clem shook her head and made a face.

"That Liam. Always Mr. Saintly."

"Clem." Dorrie's voice was reproachful.

Alec looked up from the dishwater and turned from Clem's face to Dorrie's, his eyebrows raised.

"Really," Clem asked him, her voice high, "don't you think my brother is a little hard to take sometimes?"

Alec grinned and shook his head. He let out the dishwater and dried his hands. "From Dorrie's expression, I don't think she agrees with you." His eyes were on Dorrie's face, his voice soft. "Do you, Dorrie?"

Dorrie flung her thick braid over her shoulder. She felt her face grow warm, but she kept her voice even. "I think Clem's too hard on her brother. That's all. She always has been. I feel sorry for him." *But why am I trying to deny my feelings for Liam?* she asked herself. *Why not let Alec see how I feel?* She couldn't answer the question she had asked herself; she knew only that she would like to hide as much as she could of herself from Alec's dark gaze. His eyes made her uncomfortable, as though they could see too deeply inside her, deeper than a near stranger had any right to look.

"Poor Liam," Alec said dryly. "He seems to survive, though."

Clem snorted. Dorrie bent to pet Gram's old tabby cat, hiding her face from both of them.

"I'd like to be getting home soon, Dorrie," Clem said.

"In a minute." Dorrie settled crosslegged on the kitchen floor, while the cat climbed into her lap purring. "Nice Samantha," she murmured, stroking the cat. She kept her head bent while Clem left the kitchen to tell her grandparents goodbye. For a moment she could feel Alec's eyes on her, like an itchy spot on the top of her head, but then he, too, followed Clem into the other room. "Pretty kitty," Dorrie crooned, trying to let the peculiar tension she felt flow from her hands as they stroked the limp cat.

"There you are, dear." Dorrie looked up into Gram's calm eyes. "I hope my teasing didn't make you uncomfortable."

Dorrie shrugged. "A little." Her lip curled. "But I deserved it."

Gram smiled. "I'll tell you a secret. I couldn't have answered any quizzes myself on today's sermon. I confess I was too busy watching Mason watch Clem, and you watch Liam, while Alec watched you. I hadn't realized until today what a complicated web you young people have been busy stringing. All through the service, I was trying to think of ways to help you sort it all out. Perhaps that's why I thought the text was taken from one of Paul's writings. Because eventually, the eleventh verse of the fourth chapter of First Thessalonians came into my mind quite clearly: '. . .study to be quiet.' I realized then that my planning and scheming, even my praying for what *I* wanted, was like noise coming between me and our Savior's voice."

Dorrie couldn't meet Gram's frank blue gaze.

"I won't say anything more, dear." Gram's voice was gentle. "I can see I've made you uncomfortable again. I just wanted to let you know I can see what is happening in the hearts of you young people. I won't involve myself— but I shall be quietly praying. . .for all of you." Her small hand patted Dorrie's cheek. "Come. I think the others are ready to say goodbye."

Outside, Clem climbed immediately into Dorrie's car. Dorrie hesitated, watching Liam as he said goodbye to his grandparents in the doorway. She had hoped for some new sign that he was beginning to care for her, but nothing had happened. *Alec's fault*, she thought unreasonably.

Liam came down the steps and turned to Alec. "About that situation the other day, Alec," he said. "I think you handled it all wrong."

Alec had opened his car door, but he turned now to Liam.

"Which situation was that?" he asked easily.

Liam's lips pressed together. "The one with Felix Jones in Dorrie's closet. It doesn't make sense to me—giving a kid like that extra privileges unless he's earned them."

Alec looked past Liam's face to Gram's pink roses that climbed the white trestle around the door. "Doesn't God give us good things, things we've done nothing to merit? He gives them to us not because we deserve them, but because He knows they'll help us grow, help us reach our full potential. That's how I felt about Felix and the closet. For him to be himself, the best, most creative part of Felix Jones, the part God created and longs for him to be, he desperately needs a time and place where he can be alone sometimes. Otherwise, that part of him will die."

Liam shook his head impatiently. "I don't want to get into a spiritual discussion here. I'm talking about a messed up little kid, a delinquent who could do who knows what kind of damage when he's unsupervised like that inside the school building. I'm surprised Margaret and the houseparents would ever agree to such a thing. It just doesn't make sense."

Alec looked at Liam thoughtfully. "I think both Margaret and the Corinthians Cottage houseparents recognized that this privilege is too important to Felix for him to risk losing it by abusing it. If we don't do *something* to nurture the inquisitive, creative side of Felix Jones, then it will wither up and die—and then we *will* be left with just another little delinquent." His gaze shifted to Dorrie. "What do you think, Dorrie? Felix will be in your class now. He's really not my responsibility anymore."

Dorrie hesitated. She looked from Liam's dark, impatient face to Alec's quiet gaze. From inside the car, she heard Clem make a small, disgusted noise, and Dorrie longed to put herself firmly on Liam's side. "I guess I have to agree with you," she said reluctantly to Alec. "It sounds to me as though Felix needs that closet." Her eyes went to Liam. "Though I can understand your position, too, Liam."

Liam shook his head. "You don't know, Dorrie. You haven't worked with these kids yet. You're setting yourself up for problems."

"As I said," Alec said quietly, "it's really not up to me anymore." He slid into his car and shut the door.

Liam waited until Alec had backed out of the driveway. "Anybody want to get together for pizza later?" he asked then. He bent his head to see into Dorrie's car. "Clem? How about it, Mason?"

Dorrie looked hopefully at Clem, but she shook her head violently.

"Another time, Liam," Mason muttered and climbed into his own car.

Liam looked from Mason to Clem, then met Dorrie's eyes and shrugged. He smiled, and she hugged around her the warmth of his gaze.

❧

"What's going on with those two?" he asked Dorrie the next day as they walked into the school together.

Dorrie shook her head. "I'm not sure. I guess Clem just doesn't feel it's God's will for her to marry Mason."

Liam snorted. "What did God do—send her a telegram? I love the way people blame their own decisions on what 'the Lord told them.'"

Dorrie looked at him doubtfully. "But God does show us His will. Don't you believe that?" When he didn't answer, she sighed. "I just hate to see Clem so miserable."

"She'll be all right. She's survived worse things." He held the door open for Dorrie, then touched her shoulder. "Good luck today, Dorrie. I hope your first day of classes goes well for you. Remember, be tough with the little monsters."

Dorrie stood in the hallway staring after him as he strode toward the gym. She put her hand to her shoulder, and slowly her frown turned into a smile.

Inside her own classroom, the curtains were drawn. The room was dim and quiet, but from beneath the closet door a line of light shone. She smiled and crossed the room. "Good morning, Felix," she said as she opened the closet door.

He was crouched on the floor, a piece of charcoal in his fingers, the long, gentle face of a giraffe taking shape beneath his hand. He shook back his lank, dark hair and scowled up at her. "Haven't you ever heard of knocking?"

six

"You're right," Dorrie said. "I should have knocked. Next time I'll remember."

Felix nodded curtly, then went back to his drawing. After a moment, he looked up at Dorrie again. "Well? Did you want something?"

She smiled. "Not really. Just to say hello. Your drawing is beautiful. How do you know how to draw a giraffe like that? Without looking at anything, I mean."

He shrugged. "I've been researching giraffes. At the library. Before I draw an animal, I always find out as much as I can about it, look at as many pictures as I can." His hand on the paper moved more slowly, and his voice softened. "Sometimes I try to turn into the animal." He glanced up quickly at Dorrie, then back to his picture.

Dorrie nodded seriously, knowing he had been afraid she would laugh. "Would you like to be a giraffe?"

Felix made a face. "They're too stupid. The only reason they don't get eaten by everyone is that they're so big. They're too gentle. Too quiet."

Dorrie looked up at the picture of the roaring tiger above Felix's head. "Would you rather be a tiger?"

Felix leaned closer to his drawing. "No one hurts tigers," he said after a moment. "They eat everyone else and no one eats them."

Dorrie sank down on her heels in front of the closet. She nodded. "Do you think you're like a tiger?"

He carefully drew the gentle flare of the giraffe's nostrils. He seemed almost to have forgotten Dorrie, so absorbed was he in his drawing, and she thought he would not answer her question. He smudged the charcoal line carefully with his fingertip, and then at last he said, "I'm too small."

"Too small to hurt others the way a tiger would?"

He nodded.

"But you wish you could?"

He raised his head for an instant and looked at her, his eyes flat and dark. "Of course. It's only the animals who hurt others who don't get hurt themselves."

Dorrie longed to reach out and put her hand on his small, thin shoulder. Instead, she said, "I'm not sure it works like that with people. I think maybe the people who hurt others are the ones who end up hurting themselves most of all."

His dark brows drew together, and he shook his head impatiently. Dorrie smiled. "Who is it that's hurt you, Felix?" she asked softly.

Again, he was quiet so long she was certain he would not answer. *Too fast, Dorrie, you're pushing him too fast*, she told herself, but then he whispered, so softly she could barely hear him, "My mom."

She did reach her hand toward him then, but he raised his head and scowled at her, as though warning her to come no closer. "Everyone," he added in a louder voice. "Kids like to pick on small people."

She nodded. "But think about your mom. Don't you think she hurts, too? If she didn't hurt inside, I bet she wouldn't hurt you. And I bet that after she's hurt you, she hurts inside more than ever."

His frown wrinkled his whole face, like a baby about to

cry, and then suddenly he wiped his face smooth and bent once more over his drawing. "What do you know?" he muttered.

"Not much," Dorrie admitted. "But I do know for certain that if your mom wasn't hurt inside herself, she would never hurt you. And the reason I know that, Felix Jones, is because there's no reason in the world why you should be hurt like that. *You* didn't do anything to make your mother hurt you."

"Maybe I was the one who hurt her in the first place." His voice was a whisper again.

Dorrie shook her head. "You didn't, Felix. You're not to blame for your mother being the way she is."

He was drawing the giraffe's spots now, each one different from the one before, the tip of his tongue caught between his teeth. Dorrie waited while the silence grew longer and longer, until she realized that as far as he was concerned, the conversation was over. She smiled. "You know what animal you remind me of?"

"What?" He sighed, as though humoring her.

"A snapping turtle. Because you have two ways to protect yourself. You can snap at anyone who comes too close. Or you can pull inside your own little world that you carry around with you—your art."

Felix made a face. He finished the giraffe, and then leaned back. "There."

"It's beautiful."

He glanced at her. "You kind of remind me of a giraffe, come to think of it."

"Because I'm tall?"

He nodded. "That—and you're pretty stupid, too." His dark eyes suddenly gleamed, as though he were keeping back a grin.

Dorrie smiled. "Oh yeah?"

"Yeah."

"Well," she said thoughtfully, "you may be right. I think I'm fairly gentle, too. But I'm not particularly quiet."

"No," he sighed, "you talk an awful lot." He looked past her to the clock on the wall, and his face changed, grew hard and tense again. "The others will be here soon."

Almost immediately, Dorrie heard the sound of feet in the hallway. She got to her feet, and Felix scurried to his desk, looking suddenly more like a mouse than anything else. She smiled at him, but he avoided her eyes, and she turned to the doorway to greet the other students.

As they came in, Dorrie tried to match them with their names. The girls came first, and they were easy, since she had only four of them: Tammy, her hair in a greasy ponytail, her head ducked as though she expected a blow; fat little Polly; pretty Kristen with her eyes outlined with mascara; and LaSandra, who thrust her chin forward as though daring the world to do its worst. Dorrie smiled at them, but only Polly smiled back.

She heard a sound like thunder from the hallway then. "Slow down." She recognized Alec's voice. "There's no fire that I know of."

Seven boys burst into her room. "So you're the new teacher," one of them said. "What's your name?"

"Miss Carpenter. Who are you?"

"Kenny." He sat on top of one of the desks, a big boy with a shock of straight blond hair that flopped over his forehead. "What do you think, Lamar?"

Lamar grinned shyly at Dorrie, his teeth white against his dark skin. He took a chair and did not answer Kenny.

"I think she's pretty," said a thin, freckle-faced boy.

"I like your hair," Kristen said. "Do you dye it?"

"Nope," said Dorrie. "It came that way." She caught Felix's dark stare and smiled, but he looked away quickly. She looked around the rest of the circle of students and took a deep breath, feeling as though she was about to plunge into deep water.

"Now that we're all here, let's start the day by talking to God. I'll go first, and then anyone who wants to can go next, and when we're done, I'll finish up." Dorrie closed her eyes.

"Thank You, God, for this classroom." She heard a giggle, but she kept her eyes closed. "Thank You for each one of these students. I know You love them all very much." She waited, but all she heard was more giggles and the shifting of feet. She sighed. "Thank You for being with us today. Help us to see You more clearly. In Your Son's Name, Amen."

She opened her eyes and looked around the circle of faces; all were either filled with laughter or carefully blank. "Let's get to know each other a little now. I want each of you to tell me one thing about yourself, and then one thing that you know about the person next to you on the right. I'll go first." She hesitated. "Let's see. One thing about myself. And I don't mean something you can tell just by looking at me, like I have red hair or I'm tall. Let's see." Her eye caught Felix's again, and she smiled. "I've been told recently that I like to talk. I never thought about it before, but I guess that's pretty true. I like to talk to whomever will listen to me. I like to talk even when no one at all will listen to me. Sometimes I talk to God. Sometimes I just talk to myself. I guess it's one of the important ways I handle life—by talking about it."

She turned to Kenny who sat to her right. "Now, let's see, Kenny. I just met you five minutes ago—but I could tell one thing about you as soon as you came through the door."

Kenny shook back his blond hair. "What's that?"

"You're a leader."

"What's that supposed to mean?"

LaSandra answered before Dorrie could, "It means you're good at bossing people. And she's right about that."

Kenny scowled at LaSandra and then turned to Dorrie, his eyes cold. "Somebody has to tell people what to do. Otherwise nothing happens."

Dorrie smiled. "You're absolutely right. Every group needs a leader. Being a leader is a real gift. It's also a big responsibility. Do you know what I'm talking about?"

Kenny shrugged.

"Well, suppose you got up and jumped out the window, and everyone in the class jumped right after you. That would be an example where a leader didn't use his power responsibly."

Kristen giggled. "Knowing Kenny, he'd be more likely to get up and *break* the window. And then all the boys would jump up and start breaking windows too."

Dorrie nodded. "That would be another example of a leader not being responsible."

LaSandra stuck her nose in the air. "Well, he's not my leader, that's sure. No white boy tells me what to do."

Kenny's gaze was cold and flat. "Oh yeah?"

"It's your turn, Kenny," Dorrie said hurriedly. "Tell us something about yourself."

Kenny made a face. "I don't know anything about

myself. What you see is what you get."

"What do you like to do?" Dorrie asked. "What are you good at?"

"Uh, I'm good at shooting baskets." He looked around the circle. "I bet I could beat any of you here." He grinned. "This afternoon in the gym. How about it? Who'll take me on?"

"Why don't you discuss that another time," Dorrie said. "Can you tell us something about Jamie there on the right."

Kenny looked at Jamie. "Uh, he's got curly hair."

"You're right, Kenny, he does have beautiful curly hair." The class giggled at the word beautiful, and Jamie rolled his eyes. "But can you tell us something we can't tell just by looking at Jamie?"

"Sure." Kenny grinned wickedly. "You can't tell it by looking at him, but old Jamie boy is really *dumb*."

Jamie's face turned red, and Dorrie took a deep breath. "Jamie is *not* dumb. I meant, Kenny, can you tell me something positive about Jamie?"

"You mean something good?"

"That's right."

Kenny looked at Jamie consideringly. "Nope," he said after a moment, "I can't." The class burst into laughter.

Only Felix did not laugh. His face was expressionless, but when he looked at Dorrie, his dark eyes were mocking. Again Dorrie took a breath. "Let's back up a little here. The purpose of this exercise is not to give you a chance to toss around insults. I should have specified from the beginning—I want you to tell me one good thing about yourself, and then one good thing about the person sitting on your right. Jamie, it's your turn."

By the end of the day, Dorrie was exhausted. She slumped against her desk as her students thundered from the room, leaving tipped chairs and scattered papers behind them.

"I like them," she told Clem that night. "I like them a lot. But I had this feeling all day like I was just barely in control. The kind of feeling you have when you're driving on ice. For the time being, everything's going okay. But one wrong move and—" She threw out her hands. "Disaster. It's a scary feeling."

"It was your first day," Clem said absently, as though her mind were on other things. "You'll be more comfortable with them as you get to know each other better."

Dorrie shook her head. "I kept doing stupid things. Setting myself up for situations I should have been able to avoid if I'd just thought things through better." But the last few days, she had been daydreaming about Liam, she knew, more than she had been planning for her students. She frowned. "All day long, at the last minute I'd pull things back together, get them headed back in the right direction."

"Well, that's good then," Clem said, staring at some paperwork she had brought home from the clinic.

"But it's not good, Clem. Don't you see? I don't have enough practice handling a group. My experience has all been one on one, or in small groups of three or four. I feel like a juggler trying to keep too many balls in the air at once. Sooner or later they're all going to fall and scatter all over the place."

Clem looked up from her paper and sighed. "You'll be fine, Dorrie. Just give yourself some time. I'm sure you'll find you have more confidence in yourself every day."

❧

But she didn't. Each day, Dorrie felt her muscles clenching tighter as she drove to work, as though they were preparing for a fight. Each day, her class pushed her authority a little further. One day Kenny called Felix an obscene name, loud enough for Dorrie to hear, although she pretended she hadn't. The next day John shot a paper airplane across the room. The following day she caught Kristen and LaSandra giggling and passing notes instead of working on a history project.

Through it all, Felix sat quietly. He seldom said anything to the others, and for the most part they ignored him. When he looked at Dorrie, she thought he sneered, as though he could see all too clearly the mistakes she was making.

"I'm losing them," Dorrie told Clem as they washed dishes together.

"Don't get discouraged." Clem's eyes were focused on the window, and as usual these days, her voice was preoccupied.

"I guess I just want them to like me. And I get the feeling they think I'm pretty silly."

"Of course they like you." Clem's answer sounded automatic. Dorrie stared at her, frustrated. After a moment, she threw down her dish towel and went outside.

The evening air was sharp, with a tang that smelled of fall. The late sunlight gleamed on the goldenrod in the field across the road and made the first scarlet leaves of the sumac turn brilliant. As always, everything was quiet, the only sound the faint whisper as the wind stirred the sunlit weeds. Dorrie flopped her arms in frustration, as though she could drive the quiet away, and then she ran as hard and as fast as she could up the narrow dirt road.

When she could see Alec MacIntyre's small house

through the trees, she stopped. She stood for a moment in the center of the road, panting, and then she turned and walked back. Inside the little house she shared with Clem, she knew she would find only more quiet waiting for her.

છ

"How's everything going?" The next morning, Liam came up behind her in the hallway on her way to her classroom. She had barely seen him in the past two weeks, not since the first day of school, and his absence from her life had added to the weight of her discouragement. She smiled at him now as he put a hand on her shoulder and took a step closer. "You look tired. Having problems with the monsters?"

She shook her head. "You shouldn't call them that. It just adds to your negative mind set, you know." She felt her worries disappear, though, as a glow spread from her shoulder through the rest of her body. "I'm just adjusting to the new routine," she told him. "I'm still not used to my alarm going off at six every morning. I'm glad tomorrow is Saturday so I can finally catch up on my sleep."

"I know what you mean. Listen, I've got to run, but let's get together some time soon, okay?" He squeezed her shoulder and then turned down the hallway before she could answer. She looked after him, still smiling.

"You look like you just saw God Himself," said a small, hard voice behind her.

She spun around and found Felix leaning against the wall within the shadows of a doorwell. "I haven't seen you in your closet lately," she said to him.

He shook his head. "I've been using it after school. I can use it any time that Mr. MacIntyre is in his room, and he usually works late. It's quieter in the afternoons." He frowned at Dorrie as though to let her know she was the one he was avoiding.

Dorrie opened her classroom door. "What have you been working on lately?" she asked mildly.

He glanced up at her. "Last week, it was this neat baboon from India. This week it's been field mice."

Dorrie smiled as she opened the curtains. "One of my favorites, remember?"

He shrugged. "I like the way they're put together."

Dorrie nodded. "I think God must have had fun creating the animals."

Felix flung himself into his seat. "Give me a break. Why do you have to make God a part of everything?"

"Because He just *is* a part of everything, I suppose. Come on, think how much fun you have drawing the animals. More than anyone else, God must know what it feels like to be absorbed in creation, the way you are when you're working on a drawing. He must really love you to have made you so much like Himself in that way."

Felix shook his head. "When are you going to leave?"

"You're changing the subject. What do you mean?"

"I mean, when are you going to give up and leave? I give you another month, tops."

"What are you talking about? I'm not going anywhere. My contract is for one school year. And I'm planning on being here next year, too." *Of course, I'll be here*, she thought, *this is where Liam is.*

"You'll never make it that long." He grinned, but the smile did not reach his eyes. "Hey, don't feel bad. Since I've been here, lots of teachers have come and gone. I heard the third grade teacher just quit yesterday—she didn't even make it through two weeks. And Corinthians Cottage has had two new houseparents since I came. I figure not many people are like Mr. MacIntyre." His mouth twisted. "Or like Mr. Adams either, for that matter." He shook his head at Dorrie. "I can tell. You're one of the ones who'll have enough sense to get out of this place."

Dorrie leaned against her desk and looked at Felix thoughtfully. "It must have been hard having your houseparents leave like that."

Felix shrugged. "Why should I care? They're all the same." He looked straight into Dorrie's face, as though daring her to disagree.

"Well," she said lightly, "I'm not going anywhere. I can promise you that."

"You will," he insisted. "We'll make you leave. We're good at getting rid of people."

"No." Dorrie leaned over and put her hand against the side of Felix's dark head. "No one is getting rid of me."

He shook her hand away. She thought she saw as much fear in his eyes as she did anger.

While she stood watching him, wondering what she should say next, she heard Liam's voice in the hall. She spun toward the door, smiling. "Don't forget," he called through the open doorway, "we're getting together soon."

Dorrie turned away from Felix toward her desk. The warmth from Liam's words lasted through the arrival of her other students. She smiled at them, happier than she had felt in days, listened to their chatter, and then called them to begin work on their classroom newspaper.

"Who has a piece of news for us today?"

To her surprise, Felix, who usually never said a word during class, raised his hand. "I do."

"Go on, Felix," she said, pleased he was responding to

her at last.

Felix looked around at the other students. "Miss Carpenter is in love with Mr. Adams," he announced. "I saw them kissing this morning in the hallway."

Dorrie felt her face flush. "You did not."

"I did," Felix said calmly.

"That creep?" Kenny got up from his seat and looked Dorrie up and down. "You could do better, Miss Carpenter."

Kristen had taken out a jar of nail polish and was painting her nails. "I think Mr. Adams is cute," she said without looking up.

LaSandra shook her head. "I know his sort. My mama's living with one like him. Smile real nice till they get you. Then they beat you bad."

"We're supposed to be working on a newspaper here, people," Dorrie reminded them.

"Who cares? I'm sick of this stupid class newspaper." Kenny gave John a nudge. "Bet you can't beat me arm wrestling." The other boys gathered around as Kenny and John linked hands over John's desk.

"Get back in your seats, please." Dorrie's voice was drowned by cheers from the boys as Kenny pushed over John's arm. "I said, everyone back in their seats." Her voice was louder this time.

One or two glanced at her, but now Lamar and Kenny were wrestling. Tammy joined the group of boys, giggling. Kristen and LaSandra had gone to the window and were leaning out to wave at someone in the soccer field below. Only Felix and little Polly were still in their seats. Dorrie's eyes met Felix's; he grinned, and a wave of anger washed over Dorrie.

"Get back in your seats!" she screamed.

Their heads swiveled to look at her, and they were momentarily quiet. Then they burst into laughter.

"Hey, look, everybody," Kenny shouted, "we're done with the newspaper, and now it's reading time." He went to the reading corner and began tossing books off the shelves. The other boys caught them, then shot them back at Kenny.

Kenny's arm was over his head, ready to throw another book, when he suddenly stood still and lowered his arm. Dorrie saw his eyes shift beyond her to the doorway.

"You having a party in here or what?" asked Alec MacIntyre.

seven

When the day was finally over and the students had gone back to their cottages for the weekend, Alec MacIntyre came and once more leaned against the doorway of Dorrie's classroom.

"I hope you didn't mind my interrupting like that." Two lines drew his dark brows together. He ducked his head, trying to see into Dorrie's face, but after one quick glance up, Dorrie kept her eyes fixed on the papers spread across her desk. She felt her face grow warm.

"No," she managed to say. "Obviously, I had lost control of the class."

Alec folded his long frame into one of the students' seats. "Want to talk about it?"

Not particularly, she longed to answer. She drew tiny red circles along the margin of her plan book. "I don't seem to be as good at this as I had thought I would be," she said stiffly. "I have no idea how to control them. I don't really even *want* to be 'in control' of them—I just wanted them to like me. But obviously I can't accomplish anything at all without more order. The way things are now, they don't even respect me, let alone like me."

Alec shook his head. "Respect doesn't come easy to these kids. I'm fairly certain they already like you—but respect is another thing all together for them." He tipped back in the too-small seat. "Do you like them?"

Dorrie looked up for the first time. She nodded. "I love them."

"Then you're not the failure you think you are. More than anything else—more than their need for discipline or learning—these kids need to know they're loved and accepted. That's the only way they're ever going to be able to comprehend a loving God. From talking to the kids, I think they already sense the genuine liking and concern you have for them." His dark eyes met hers, and he smiled. "Next question: do *you* respect *them*?"

"I think so."

Alec nodded. "I could tell from the way you interacted with Felix that day before classes started that you saw him as a person in his own right. These kids aren't objects put here for our pleasure or convenience. Before God, we and our students are equals. Agreed?"

How condescending he is, she thought, but she swallowed her resentment and nodded.

"Then can you respect and love these kids enough to set aside your own selfish need to be liked?"

Dorrie gripped her red pen until her knuckles turned white. "What do you mean?" She saw his eyes drop to her hand, and a small corner of his lip curled; she forced her fingers to relax.

"I'm sorry," he said, his voice suddenly very soft. "Am I being insufferable?"

Their eyes met. Dorrie felt her own face grow hot again, even as she was surprised to see the red that tinged Alec's high cheek bones. "I always say the wrong thing to you in the wrong way, don't I?" He shook his head, then ran a hand through his hair. The thick curls stood on end even after his hand was gone, as though his hair was made of wire. For the first time, she nearly smiled.

She saw his eyes note the change in her expression, and his own face relaxed a little. She shifted in her chair; she had never met anyone so sensitive to each tiny change in her face and muscles, and for a moment she had the sensation of being examined under a microscope.

He cleared his throat. "I've been working here six years now, but when I started I was just like you. I interacted with the kids the way I would have if they had been people I'd met socially—my main goal was to make them like me. They *did* like me—and for a year or so, I was too self-centered to understand that wasn't enough.

"Eventually, it occurred to me that as a follower of Christ, I was also supposed to be an imitator of Christ. Christ didn't come to earth to make people like Him. He wasn't the sort of one-man-show that I had been trying to be. Instead, I think a lot of the time He was quiet, and He listened. When He did speak, He spoke directly to people's needs.

"When I realized that, I saw that I couldn't put myself at the center of my relationship with the kids. I have to put God there instead. When I finally did that, I saw that one of the things these kids desperately need is the security of a sense of order, a system of checks and balances. Most of their home lives have lacked that, so they behave like a ball bouncing wildly back and forth, up and down, trying to see if there are any limits. If we love them and respect them, then I think it's our job to set the limits, the boundary lines of what's acceptable behavior." With one long finger, he traced a name scored into the desk by some past student. "I know you have the school rules posted on the wall like the rest of us—but have you established any classroom rules?"

Dorrie shook her head. Her sense of her own foolishness added to her resentment. *Anyone who can talk as long as he can obviously missed his calling as a minister,* she thought.

Alec's eyes were on his hands, and he seemed unaware of her discomfort. "You might think about coming up with a set of ten or so rules. Do it with the kids. Your job will be to help them keep it short and pertinent. Otherwise, they'll include everything from not wiping your nose on your sleeve to saying, 'Excuse me,' when you burp. And for each rule there should be a consequence that will occur if the rule is broken, as well as if it is followed." He looked up at her. "If you'd like to use a system of tokens and rewards, maybe we could combine our classes on Fridays for some special activity. A movie maybe, or a picnic, or a trip into town. What do you think?"

She swallowed. *I know this; I knew everything he told me. So why wasn't I doing it? Why did I set myself up for this whole depressing situation?* "I—I guess so," she said out loud.

"Believe me, things get a lot simpler when you have a structure to work inside. You're merely enforcing rules they made themselves—and you don't have that uneasy feeling that things are creeping more and more out of hand."

In spite of herself, Dorrie's gaze met his, and she smiled. "I've had that feeling a lot ever since classes started." She set her red pen down on the desk and sighed. "Thanks, Alec," she made herself say. "You've been a big help."

"I'm glad." She felt his eyes resting on her face. "And I'm glad you've finally put down that pen. For a while there, I was afraid you were going to stab me with it."

She grinned, but looked away from the smile in his eyes. "I've got to get home." She stood up and reached for her briefcase. Her sleeve brushed the red pen and sent it rolling to the floor; she bent to pick it up at the same time he reached for it. Their arms bumped, and she felt his warmth. Strands of her red hair caught on the wool of his sweater, and she put up her hand to smooth her head as she stood up quickly. She heard his breath catch and glanced down into his face.

"Sorry," he said, but for once he was not looking at her; instead, his lashes lay in dark half-circles against his cheeks. He stood up and put his hands in his pockets. "I'd better be getting home, too."

Dorrie looked after him; in spite of herself, she found herself noticing the breadth of his shoulders beneath his sweater, the length of his legs within the casual corduroys he always wore. She shrugged and turned back to her desk to pack up her briefcase.

❧

As she came out of the school building, she caught a glimpse of Liam's dark head disappearing into his truck. She walked faster, hoping he would at least wave as he pulled out of the parking lot, but by the time she had reached her own car, his truck was gone. She sighed and drove home slowly. For the moment, she forgot her class, forgot Alec MacIntyre with his pushy good advice, and thought only of Liam. *Please, God, let something happen between us soon.*

When she pulled into the dirt road, in the distance she could see Clem's car already in their driveway, with Mason's car parked behind. She smiled to herself, certain she would find them snuggled on the sofa, their differences resolved.

But when she went through the front door, singing "Amazing Grace" loudly to let them know she was coming, she found Mason standing just inside the door, while Clem leaned against the kitchen counter, her shoulders stiff.

"Oh, come on, you two," Dorrie laughed. "Can't you just kiss and make up?"

"It's not that simple, Dorrie." Clem's voice was small and tight.

Mason threw out his hands helplessly. "I give up. Let me know if you change your mind, Clem. In the meantime, I won't bother you anymore." He glanced at Dorrie. "Nice to see you, Dorrie. I'd better be going, though."

Dorrie waited until the door closed behind him, then turned to Clem. "Come on, Clemmie, can't you see how miserable you're making the both of you? How can this be God's will for you? He wants us to be happy, remember?"

Clem's lips pressed into a tight line. "He wants us to follow Him. To take up our cross and follow Him. I don't think He necessarily said anything about being happy."

"But He did. Remember in John 16—'ask, and you shall receive, that your joy may be full'?"

Clem shook her head. She turned her back to Dorrie and stood staring out the kitchen window. "Grow up, Dorrie." Dorrie had never heard Clem's voice sound so hard. "We don't get all the things we selfishly want. That's not what Christ meant. In fact, more often than not, the thing we think we want most is the very thing God will ask us to give up. I learned that a long time ago when Mom and Dad died. Maybe the joy comes later—but that's different from the selfish happiness that comes from having your own way." She turned around and met Dorrie's gaze, her blue eyes cool and level. "Maybe it's time you thought about that in connection with Liam, Dorrie."

Dorrie stared at her. Suddenly, Clem's eyes softened, then filled with tears. "I'm sorry, Dorrie. Forget I said that. I just need to be alone for a while."

Dorrie took a step closer to her. "Remember when I first came? You said that whatever happened with Mason, it would be easier because you and I would be together."

Clem brushed her hand across her eyes and nodded.

"Well, don't you think it might help if you just talked about all this with me? You've been shutting yourself off not only from Mason, but from me, too. I feel as confused as he must. It just doesn't make sense to me."

Clem's hands clenched at her sides. "I'm sorry, Dorrie. But this isn't something that it would do any good to talk about. I'm quite certain I can't marry Mason. I'm afraid I'd rather be alone while I learn to deal with that. Please try to understand." Her voice was thick with unshed tears; she rushed across the room and shut her bedroom door behind her.

Dorrie looked after her, then sighed and went to change from her school clothes into jeans and a sweater. When she came out of her room, Clem's door was still closed. As always, the little house was very quiet. Dorrie made a face and went outside to sit beneath the giant oak.

She leaned back against its solid bulk and stretched her legs out in the grass. Two people had told her she was selfish today. A russet oak leaf drifted down into her lap; she ran her finger along its lobes and tried to piece Clem's words together with Alec MacIntyre's. *Am I selfish, God?* Her mind raced in circles from thoughts of her class to Liam and back again, from Alec MacIntyre to Clem and Mason and back once more to Liam. *Liam. . . .*

"Dor-riee!" called Clem's voice from the house. "Telephone!"

Dorrie scrambled to her feet, her heart suddenly thudding. "It's my mother, right?" she asked Clem as she raced through the door.

Clem made a face and shook her head. She handed Dorrie the telephone.

"Dorrie?" said Liam's voice, and her heart pounded still harder. "I hope I didn't interrupt anything."

"No. No. I was just—I was just outside. Hi, Liam." She felt her mouth stretching into a smile so wide it hurt her cheeks, and she saw Clem roll her eyes before she went back into her room.

"We promised to get together soon, remember?" said Liam's light voice in her ear, "and since it's Friday night, I was wondering if you were doing anything? I know it's the last moment, but I thought maybe we could get something to eat, maybe see a movie. You know—go out on a real date."

eight

"You promised me you'd pray about it before you went out with Liam." Clem's voice was small and hard.

Dorrie whirled away from the telephone, still smiling. "Oh, Clem, can't you see? This *is* an answer to prayer." She hugged Clem's stiff shoulders. "He asked me out! Why, just today, on the way home, I was praying—" She twirled around Clem, feeling as though her every muscle were jingling with joy. Clem looked at her, not smiling. "Come on, Clemmie, please. Be just a little happy for me, can't you? You know this is what I've wanted for years."

"It's just a date, Dorrie. Don't make more out of it than it is."

"You should talk, Clem. You're the one acting as though I've done something dangerous and immense." Dorrie hugged herself. "But in a way you're right. I know it's a beginning. I know it is. I *know* this is God's hand in my life."

"How can you be so sure?"

"I just feel it inside. You know—a kind of certainty." Dorrie stopped twirling and looked at Clem. "I suppose," she said slowly, "the same way you're so sure God *doesn't* want you to marry Mason." For a moment they stared at each other. Then both looked away.

"Oh, come on, Clem. Help me decide what to wear."

❧

Clem refused to help her, but Dorrie finally decided on a

dark green crushed velvet top that hung down over black leggings. Her green eyes stared back at her from the mirror, as she gave her red hair one last brush. "Please, God," she whispered, "let him like the way I look."

She heard Liam's truck in the driveway and dashed out of the bathroom. "Bye," she called into Clem's room and ran out the door.

Liam's blue eyes glowed when she slid into the truck beside him. "You look beautiful, Dorrie," he said softly.

Dorrie forced herself to lean back against the seat, to relax her legs, her arms, her hands. "Thank you," she whispered.

"How's my sister?" he asked as he turned the truck around.

Dorrie let out her breath in a sigh. "Gloomy. I've never seen her like this. I don't understand her."

Liam's eyes were steady on the road ahead. "Clem and I have never been the chummy sort of brother and sister," he said after a moment, "but I think I can guess why she's thinking the way she is. Maybe I should talk to her sometime."

Dorrie turned to him. "I wish you would. She's just making herself miserable. And everyone around her, too. I know you could help her."

Liam smiled. "Little Dorrie. You always have such confidence in me."

Dorrie grinned. "I do have confidence in you. But I'm hardly little."

Liam shrugged. "I always see you the way you looked the first time I talked with you. You were so young then, you made me hurt inside." He smiled at her sideways. "All long legs and big eyes, like a fawn or a foal."

Oh, Father, he remembers the first time he talked to me. Dorrie remembered too; she had fallen in love with him by the end of that first conversation.

Liam shook his head. "I'm afraid your confidence is misplaced this time, though. I'm not very good at counseling people. And Clem's always been the spiritual giant of the family. She probably wouldn't listen to anything I had to say anyway. She knows me too well."

"What do you mean?"

He grimaced. "Oh, Clem's always seen through me pretty well. She probably knows my weaknesses better than I do myself." He glanced at Dorrie. "I bet she's filled you in on them, too, hasn't she?"

Dorrie shifted her legs, stared out the window at the lights of the town they were approaching, and then set her lips firmly. "I don't listen to her."

Liam laughed; Dorrie smiled and turned toward him. "Well, look at the way she's acting now about Mason. I love her dearly—but sometimes her perceptions are obviously—well, warped, I guess."

Liam laughed again. "Meaning, I guess, that on the one hand my fears about my sister's opinion of me have just been confirmed—but on the other hand, you've relieved me considerably."

Dorrie looked at him shyly. "Why?"

"Because," he answered softly, "what you think about me is important to me, little Dorrie. I think I'd rather you didn't see me too clearly."

Maybe I see you more clearly than anyone else. The words hung on her lips, unsaid. She looked at the side of his dark, bearded face, the straight angles of his jaw and nose, the curve of his small, neat ear, the sleek shine of his hair, and she felt as though she might burst from loving him. He turned his head and smiled at her; the look in his eyes seemed to say he understood what she was still too shy to say out loud.

They ate at a quiet restaurant converted from an old Victorian home. A fire crackled on the hearth next to them, and candles caught the blue lights in Liam's black hair. "You're even prettier in candlelight," he said softly.

Dorrie felt his eyes on her. She looked down at her food and struggled for something intelligent to say. "How is work going for you?" she asked at last.

He reached across the table and lay a finger against her lips. "Shh. Don't mention that place. Not tonight. Tonight is magic."

Her mouth burned where he had touched her. The silence stretched between them, but she no longer minded. Whenever she met his eyes, they seemed full of messages too special for words. *For once,* she thought, *I don't mind the quiet. I can be still with Liam, see that, God? I don't have to talk, and neither does he, not like Alec MacIntyre. That must show that our spirits are close in You, Father, don't You think? I could look at him forever, and never notice the quiet at all. Oh, Father, thank You for tonight.*

"What are you thinking?"

"Oh," she lowered her eyes to the cup of tea in her hand. "Nothing much. I was just appreciating the quiet."

"That's something I've always liked about you, Dorrie— your ability to be quiet. I'm never comfortable with people who talk too much. Whenever I'm with someone who chatters, I find myself soon itching to be somewhere else."

She raised her eyes from her teacup. "I talk a lot sometimes, Liam," she had to say. *Are You changing me*

*into a whole new sort of person, Father? Or does Liam
see a part of me that even I don't know?*

He smiled. "Dorrie, I've known you for years now, and
I've never known you to be anything but quiet and peaceful."

She returned his smile doubtfully. She had always been
tongue-tied around him, overwhelmed by her feelings for
him; that was the reason for her quietness around him, she
knew, but perhaps she could cultivate a new, truer stillness
in her soul.

At the movie theater, she stared at the flickering screen,
but her thoughts circled round and round this new quietness she must learn to develop. *Isn't that what everyone
has been saying to me lately, God? Even Alec MacIntyre,
hadn't said something about being still? And so had Gram,
and so had Margaret Truesdell. Even the house. Maybe
the reason I've been noticing the quiet so much is because You were trying to get a message through to me.
You knew what Liam needed and You were trying to get
me ready. I wasn't comfortable with the quiet before,
because I didn't understand, but now I do, and oh, God,
thank You so much for this night. I'm ready to change in
whatever way I need to so that I can be the sort of woman
Liam needs.*

She closed her eyes, chattering on and on to God about
this new quietness she knew was about to blossom inside
her, until she felt Liam move beside her. In the darkness,
his hand reached toward her. His warm slender fingers
linked with hers, and her thoughts were scattered; for the
rest of the evening, the messages from her excited body
blocked out all other sound.

ಖ

"So how was it?" Clem was curled up on the sofa reading when Dorrie came through the door.

"It was wonderful." Dorrie smiled. "Were you waiting up for me, Mother?"

Clem made a face. "Yes, I was. I wanted to talk to you."

Dorrie glanced at Clem's serious eyes, and she sighed. "Couldn't we wait until tomorrow? I already know what you think about your brother, I know you're not happy I went out with him, I know you're not happy about anything right now. But I am. I just want to go to bed and be quiet."

Clem looked at her. "Are you okay? You, Dorrie Carpenter, 'just want to be quiet'? This I thought I'd never hear."

Dorrie looked down at her hand, the hand Liam had held for the remainder of the movie, and smiled. "I'm going to change, Clem, I'm already changing. I'm going to learn to be a quiet person."

Clem snorted, then burst into laughter. "I'll believe that when I see it. Come on, Dorrie, what's brought this on?" She stared at Dorrie's dreamy face, and then she grimaced. "Not Liam. Please tell me you're not going to try to change yourself for Liam."

Dorrie moved around the room, stretching her long legs after sitting still all evening. "Isn't that what people do for the people they love?"

"No. They don't." Clem put her head in her hands. "Honestly, Dorrie, this thing with Liam is getting worse and worse. It's like you're bewitched. You don't see Liam the way he really is. You think you do, but I know you don't. That was bad enough. But now you want to make him see you some way that you're really not. Don't you see, even if you could have a relationship, even if Liam wants that, it wouldn't be *real*?"

Dorrie shook her head. "I don't want to make him *see* me a way that I'm not. I want to *be* the way he needs me to be."

"Oh, please, Dorrie, Liam doesn't need you to be anything. He wants you to fall in love with him, I'll grant you that. I see the way he looks at you, and it's the same old pattern. I've watched him do it ever since he was a teenager. He likes to make girls love him. Maybe it's because he's insecure inside, maybe it comforts the scared little boy who felt abandoned when Mom and Dad died. But whatever the reason, he uses girls to make himself feel good, and then he hurts them. Because I'm warning you, Dorrie, Liam isn't looking for a serious relationship. The sooner he's certain you've fallen for him, the sooner he'll drop you and move on to someone else. That's just the way he is."

"No," Dorrie shouted, suddenly angry, "you're wrong! You're just jealous because you can't let yourself be happy with Mason. You don't believe God wants anyone to be happy." She stared at Clem for a moment longer, her cheeks like fire, and then she flung herself out the door. She ran up the dark road, her feet thudding, her breath loud, filling the still, cold night with her own angry noise.

❧

For the rest of the weekend, Dorrie and Clem were careful and polite with each other. At church on Sunday, Liam sat beside Dorrie, and she missed yet another of Grandpop Adams' sermons. She felt Clem's level gaze on her as she stood talking with Liam after the service, but she ignored her friend, and kept her eyes on Liam. Between the black of his hair and beard, his blue eyes blazed; looking into them, she tried to let him see the new quietness unfolding within her.

"I'll see you tomorrow," he said. She looked after his straight back, then turned to retrieve her Bible from the pew where she had left it. As she reached between the pews, she barely noticed she had brushed against someone, until she heard Alec MacIntyre's voice.

"Hello, Dorrie," he said quietly.

"Oh, sorry," she said, "I didn't see you."

He nodded gravely. "I'm easy to miss. It's my petite stature, I suppose."

She smiled reluctantly. "I guess my mind was just on other things."

He nodded. The look on his face made her shift her feet and inch toward the aisle. *But he can't know how I feel about Liam. And I wouldn't care if he did.*

"Was your mind so busy that you missed who came to church with me?"

She looked up at him. "I guess it must have been. Who did you bring to church?"

"The last person you might expect. He called me up this morning, said he wanted to try another church besides the chapel at the Home." Alec grinned. "His exact words actually were, 'I want to see if one is any less stupid than the other.'"

"Not Felix Jones?"

Alec nodded. "He's waiting out in my car."

"I can't believe I didn't see him."

"Like you said, Dorrie, your mind was on other things. I don't think you looked our way once."

Dorrie's cheeks grew warm, but before she could

answer, Alec continued, "I'm giving Felix dinner out at my place." He shrugged his shoulders, and she noticed the warm color along the high bones of his cheeks. "He said I should ask you to join us."

She stared at him, forgetting her embarrassment. "Felix said that? I had the impression the last time I saw him Friday that he would just as soon never see me again. He wouldn't even look at me."

"Maybe he's had a change of heart." He smiled. "Come on out to my car. Let's see."

She followed him out of the church to the car that was as small and old as her own. Inside, Felix sat waiting, his fingers tapping on the door. When he saw Dorrie, he scowled and rolled down the window. "Are you going to come?"

Dorrie looked from him to Alec, and then her eyes went back to Felix. She nodded. "I'll come." She turned to Alec. "Clem drove today, and I think she's going to her grand-parents' for dinner. You'll have to give me a ride."

He smiled. "I think we can handle that."

Felix made a face. "His back seat is full of cat hairs. I suppose that means we'll all have to sit in the front. But I'm not sitting in the middle. I get claustrophobic."

Dorrie ran to let Clem know where she was going. She ignored the pleased expression on her friend's face and turned back to Alec's car. She took a deep breath and reminded herself she was doing this for the sake of her relationship with Felix, and then she climbed into the middle of the front seat.

They said very little on the short drive back to Alec's house. Alec seemed to be concentrating on the road, while Felix's head was turned toward the side window. Dorrie stared straight ahead feeling smothered. She did not mind the warmth of Felix's small shoulder on her right side, but the heat from Alec's big body on her left annoyed her. She shifted uncomfortably, trying to squeeze closer to Felix.

"Stop squashing me," he said crossly.

"I'm sorry." She turned toward him. "We had a terrible day Friday. I'm glad you wanted me to come today."

His head turned and his eyes behind their thick lenses glared at her. "Is that what he told you?" He leaned forward so he could see Alec's face, and then he smiled smugly. "I told him to ask you because I like to make life harder for Mr. Adams."

"What do you mean?"

Alec cleared his throat loudly, but Felix's eyes gleamed, and he said, "Both Mr. Adams and Mr. MacIntyre are obviously hot for you. I may be betting on the underdog, but my money's on Mr. MacIntyre."

nine

"That was not a socially appropriate comment." Alec's voice was calm and level. He drove past Dorrie and Clem's house, and up the road to his own small house.

Felix smirked. "You can't deny it is true, though, can you, Mr. MacIntyre?"

"That's really not any of your business, Felix," Alec said pleasantly. He parked the car in his driveway. "Come on, you two. I am about to impress you both with my amazing skill in the kitchen."

Dorrie followed Felix out of the car, but she was thinking about Alec's words on Friday, when he had compared the students to bouncing balls looking for their limits. Felix had tried to bounce high and fast, just as he had in her classroom on Friday; Alec, however, had neatly caught the ball and quietly, but firmly, sent it back within its limits. She followed his tall figure up the path through the trees to his house, then hurried to catch up with him. "You handled that well," she murmured as he opened his door.

He glanced at her sideways, and the corner of his mouth curved. "I'm glad you thought so."

As she followed him through the door, she looked at him curiously and saw that the tips of his ears were red. *Can Alec MacIntyre really be attracted to me, God?* She pushed the uncomfortable thought away, and bent to pet the ginger cat that was rubbing against her leg. "This must be Esther."

Alec nodded. "That," he said to Felix, pointing to the cat, "is the only woman in my life." He grinned. "For all our sakes, please remember that in the future."

"Sure," Felix muttered. He knelt beside the cat and watched her. "I had a cat once." He held out his hand carefully and let Esther sniff his fingers.

Dorrie looked around the small house, noticing the stacks of books everywhere, then settled on the floor beside Felix. "Mr. MacIntyre seems to use his chairs as receptacles for books. Apparently he hasn't heard of shelves." She smiled at Felix. "What was your cat's name?"

"Sam. He got run over by a car."

Dorrie watched the careful way Felix touched Esther. "I'm sorry."

He shrugged. "Animals are always getting run over at the trailer court where I live. They're so stupid, they sleep in the road. Some guy has too much beer and peels out without looking—" He shrugged again. "I saw a squashed dog one time. You could see its intestines."

Alec pulled a mixing bowl out of the cupboard. "Thank you, Felix," he said over his shoulder, "but descriptions of dead animals are generally also inappropriate topics for polite conversation."

Felix made a face. "'Inappropriate.' 'Polite.' Who cares? You people need to face the real world."

Alec broke an egg into the bowl. "What exactly is the 'real' world?"

Felix lay on his stomach, his chin on his hands, and stared at Esther. "Come visit my mom at the trailer court. That place is what reality is all about. You guys at the Home, that old guy talking at church today, you're all living in fantasy land."

Alec reached into the refrigerator and brought out a package of chicken cutlets. "There are all kinds of realities, Felix," he said. "With the amount of reading you do, I know you already know there's a whole world outside the trailer court." He began dipping the cutlets into the egg, then rolled them in bread crumbs. "I happen to believe that the things that are most truly 'real' are found in God. A lot of the other stuff, whether you find it at the trailer court or in the politest society in the world, is just lies."

Felix scowled. "That's what I mean—fantasy land. You don't want to accept reality, so you pretend it's not there." He looked up at Alec over his glasses. "Sorry, Mr. MacIntyre, but people out there hurt each other and use each other. That's real life. The trailer court's not pretty, but at least it doesn't pretend life's about some fantasy super-hero who runs everything, the way you do."

Dorrie leaned back on her hands, and waited while Alec dropped the meat into a hot frying pan. He ran water into a kettle, and set it on the stove, and she noticed how calm his face was, how efficient and unhurried his movement around the kitchen. She put her hand on Esther's warm fur, and a strange sort of peace settled over her. *How odd,* she thought, for the quiet calm inside her heart felt unfamiliar and yet comfortable. She closed her eyes, absorbing through her fingers Esther's quiet purr while she listened to Felix's and Alec's voices.

"Christ is bigger than a super-hero," Alec was saying now. "Use that marvelous brain we hear so much about and read some of the new physics. Even in the midst of chaos, there's more beauty and order than our small minds ever dreamed." Dorrie heard the clatter of a pan, but she felt the stillness around her absorb the noise, undisturbed.

"And when I said a lot of the other stuff in the world is lies," Alec went on, "I meant it's based on lies." She heard him beat something with a spoon. "For instance, it's a lie that we need anything out there to make us happy and complete, whether it's sex or drugs or money or whatever. We think we do—and that's why we use people, and people end up hurt."

The cat purred; the oven door creaked open and shut; the water in the kettle began to bubble and spatter; Dorrie was almost asleep. "St. Augustine said that all of us strive for unending happiness, but our hearts are restless until they rest in God," Alec said. "T.S. Elliot called God the still point of the turning world. And James in the Bible calls Him the Father of lights who has no shadow of turning." The refrigerator door opened and closed. "It's that stillness, that security, that we all need. Only when we find it can we truly rest. And that, Felix, in more words than you ever wanted to hear," Dorrie heard the smile in Alec's voice, "is what I believe about reality."

"What about Sleeping Beauty here?" asked Felix. "I bet she thinks she needs Mr. Adams in order to be happy. I see the way she looks at him."

Dorrie opened her eyes, the quietness shattered. She looked up and met Alec's gaze. "We're all still human," he said gently, but something about his voice made her think he was talking about himself more than her. She turned away from the wistfulness in his eyes and looked at Felix.

He was lying on his stomach, nose to nose with Esther, but his dark eyes skewed in her direction. "You going to marry Mr. Adams, Miss Carpenter?"

Dorrie hesitated. She looked at Alec, but his eyes were now on the frying pan, and he did not look up again. She knew he was listening, though, and she found herself reluctant to answer Felix's question. *I am going to marry Liam, aren't I, God?* But of course she could not tell Felix that, when Liam himself did not know it yet. She shifted uncomfortably, feeling her old restlessness come over her. "I don't know," she said at last, reluctantly.

Felix laughed. "She doesn't know. What's that mean?"

Alec turned from the stove. "You don't have to answer him, you know, Dorrie." His dark eyes were clouded, but his voice was gentle. "There's no reason that our students have to know every intimate detail of our personal lives. As I reminded Felix earlier, it's really none of their business." Dorrie heard the message in his voice; she realized she had been thinking of Felix as that social acquaintance who she wanted to like her, rather than keeping the distance that needed to be between a student and teacher.

Alec grinned and leaned across to flick the top of Felix's head with his fingertips. "Sorry, Felix, no matter how much we love you, we're not going to lay out our love lives for you to examine."

The corners of Felix's mouth turned down. "Right. Like you really love me."

Dorrie smiled. "Well, we do."

Felix squirmed. After a moment, though, he looked sideways at her again and grinned evilly. "As much as you love Mr. Adams?"

Dorrie grabbed a book from the nearest stack and leaned over to smack Felix gently on the head with it. "Enough!"

Felix giggled, and for the first time since she'd met him, Dorrie thought he looked like an eleven-year-old boy, his expression no longer hard and guarded.

Alec pulled a loaf of warm bread from the oven. "Here, Dorrie," he said, "make yourself useful and slice this for me. And you, Felix," he reached across the table and pulled a piece of paper and a pencil from beneath another pile of books, "take this and draw me a picture of Esther while we finish getting this meal on the table. Maybe that will occupy that busy little brain of yours long enough to give Dorrie and me some peace." He smiled.

Felix grabbed the paper and pencil and put it on the floor in front of him. He wiggled back away from Esther a few inches, and then, still lying on his stomach, began to sketch the gentle curve of the cat's back. Dorrie watched for a second, then turned to take the bread knife from Alec's hand.

The kitchen work space was small; Dorrie found herself brushing against Alec every time she moved. "Sorry," she muttered when they jumped away after running into each other yet again. *It's no big deal*, she told herself. She felt nervous and on edge, though, and for the first time, she wished she had gone with Clem to her grandparents'. Maybe Liam would have come over, too, and right now she could have been with him, instead of here with this man who was so large she could barely breathe without touching him.

She remembered then the quietness she had felt for a few moments, and she thought smugly, *You're already changing me into the quiet person Liam needs, aren't You, God?* She wished she had been with Liam when she had experienced it, instead of wasting the moment on Alec MacIntyre.

"This is obviously a one-person kitchen," Alec said. He smiled, but his voice was oddly breathless. "Why don't you go sit down. I can manage the rest."

Dorrie moved gratefully away from the kitchen area. "Where do you suggest I sit?" She looked at the dining room table spread with papers and books, all but one of the chairs piled with still more books.

"Improvise," Alec answered.

Dorrie began piling up the books and papers on the table, glancing at the book titles as she did so. Besides several different versions of the Bible, Alec seemed to be reading five novels, two documentaries, three scientific books, an autobiography, a history book, and four inspirational books, all simultaneously.

In spite of herself, Dorrie smiled. She looked at the books thoughtfully, realizing that most of them were either favorites of hers or books she had been wanting to read. "I don't have to ask what you do with your spare time," she said lightly. She took the books off the chairs and stacked them on the floor against the wall.

Alec set a bowl of spaghetti and pesto on the table. "I guess you could say that those are my companions." He nodded toward the stacks of books. "Esther's nice, but she doesn't talk much. Living by myself, my mind tends to get a little hyperactive if I don't have someone else's thoughts and ideas to act as a balance. When I first lived alone, I felt so restless, I thought I'd go crazy. Then I started inviting friends over." He reached for one of the books. "This one's by C.S. Lewis—a very good friend."

Dorrie turned to look at him. He was closer behind her than she had thought, but for once she did not jump away. She found herself looking up into his eyes, absently noticing the way they slanted above his high cheekbones. "Even though I live with Clem," she heard herself say, "sometimes I feel as though I might as well be living alone. Things are a little hard with her right now." She paused, surprised she was telling him this. "The house seems so quiet. I feel like I can't stand it sometimes." She reached for the plates he had set on the counter and began putting them on the table. She glanced up at him quickly. "Usually, I like to read too. But lately even that seems too quiet. I'm always running out of the house, trying to escape."

He nodded. "I see you on the road sometimes. Running." He moved away, reaching for the glasses from the cupboard. "Learning to be quiet can be uncomfortable sometimes," he said over his shoulder. "I think it's because only in stillness can we hear God's voice—and God's voice isn't always a comfortable thing. We're like Jonah, running away, insisting on our own way." He handed her the glasses and took silverware from a drawer. "Must have been awfully quiet inside that whale. No one to talk to, nowhere to run. Jonah had to finally face himself—and God."

He came around the table to set the silverware beside the plates, and Dorrie again pulled back from his closeness. *You're like a whale yourself, Alec MacIntyre—huge and threatening, chasing me down when I just want to escape.* She giggled nervously at her thoughts, then shook her head when Alec looked at her questioningly. *Just leave me alone. Stop following me with your eyes. Stop noticing my every expression, my every thought.* She moved to the other side of the table; she knew he would have noted her movement and probably guessed that she was trying to distance herself from him, but she refused to look at him again.

The awkwardness between them eased when Felix joined them at the table. He waited impatiently while Alec gave thanks for the food, then raised his eyebrows in pretended disbelief as he looked at the plates of food. "Green spaghetti?"

"Pesto," Alec told him.

"Yuck."

"Expand your horizons," Dorrie said. "It's delicious. Everything is." She smiled at Alec, though she avoided meeting his eyes.

Felix took a forkful of spaghetti. "Not bad," he admitted. "Of course anything's better than the slop they feed us over at the Home."

"I think," Alec said, "if I read between the lines, I can interpret that as, 'Thank you for inviting me for dinner, Mr. MacIntyre. I really appreciate the home-cooked meal.' Am I right?"

Felix shrugged, sucking in a long strand of spaghetti. "I guess."

Dorrie found herself exchanging glances with Alec over Felix's head. They smiled, and suddenly the uneasiness inside her relaxed; once again, she felt that odd sense of comfortable peace. "So, Felix," she said, "tell me when you started drawing."

The rest of the meal passed easily. Felix told them stories about life in the trailer court, and Dorrie found herself laughing with Alec until their eyes watered; other times, she felt her eyes burn with unshed tears as she listened to Felix.

When they had finished eating, she and Felix did the dishes. Felix washed and managed to spill quantities of water on the floor, while Esther retreated to the top of the refrigerator to watch. Alec leaned against the kitchen table behind them; Dorrie felt his eyes on her, and now and then she glanced over her shoulder at him and smiled. She could not explain the change in her feelings, as though a door inside her had first opened, then slammed shut, and now stood open again; she only knew that her heart felt quiet and content, as though she were resting close to God.

She and Felix finished the last dish. "How about a game of Monopoly?" Alec asked.

Felix groaned. "I despise Monopoly. It's the most boring game ever invented."

"It's the only game I own, though," Alec answered.

"I know," Dorrie said, "let's play the dictionary game. I know you must have a dictionary somewhere, Alec, and I'm sure Felix will be good at making up definitions." She explained the rules of the game.

Again, Dorrie found herself laughing till tears ran down her cheeks at Felix's and Alec's crazy and creative definitions. She could not remember when she had last felt so relaxed, so simply happy. When Alec announced that the time had come to take Felix back to the Home, she was disappointed to have the afternoon end.

She hesitated in the doorway of Alec's house, giving Esther one last stroke along her back. She felt strangely reluctant to leave, as though she knew the magic spell would end once she left Alec's cluttered little house, and she would be back to being her old restless self; that door inside her would slam shut again, separating her from the warmth she saw in Alec's eyes.

What am I thinking? She backed out of the door quickly. "Did you want your drawing of Esther?" she asked Felix.

He shrugged. "Mr. MacIntyre can have it."

"Thank you, Felix," Alec said. "Maybe I can have it framed."

"Right," Felix said sarcastically.

"Seriously," Alec answered. "It's a very good drawing. It means a lot to me that you gave it to me. I've always wished I could have one of your drawings."

Felix shrugged. He too seemed to be changing back into his old self, pulling his defenses tight around him once more.

"Want me to drop you at your house?" Alec asked Dorrie as they walked out to his car.

Dorrie shook her head. "I think I'll walk home." She smiled at Felix. "I'll see you tomorrow, Felix. I enjoyed being with you this afternoon very much." She glanced quickly at Alec. "Thank you for dinner. It was a nice time."

He nodded. "It was." He opened his mouth as though to say something more, then closed it again. "I'll see you," was all he said at last.

Dorrie waved as his car pulled away, and then walked slowly home. *I should have been with Liam this afternoon*, she thought, but then she remembered Felix's giggles when he had stumped her at the dictionary game. She smiled.

As she walked along the quiet road, she felt God's presence with her. "Thank You, God," she began, and then found she had no more words, and so she said again, "Thank You." She listened to the small sounds of the wind blowing leaves across the road, a crow cawing in the oak trees overhead, and the crunch of her own feet in the gravel along the shoulder of the road. "Thank You," she whispered once more, and then the door inside her heart swung open wide, welcoming His quiet presence.

ىa

Her sense of peace lasted through the evening and was still with her as she drove to the Home the next morning. She was planning how to set up her classroom rules as she swung into the parking lot. "Please help me," she whispered to God, and then got out of her car.

She noticed Alec's car in the parking lot, and her step quickened, for she hoped that this morning Felix might be in his closet in her room. She had found herself thinking about him again and again during the night, wishing she could give him a different sort of life than the one he had experienced so far. *He's so smart and funny, so hungry to be loved*, she thought as she went in the school building. *Alec talks to him so easily about You, God. Please give me opportunities to show him Your love too. What I really wish, God, is that I could take him home and show him what it's like to be loved and secure. If Liam and I get married, then maybe we could adopt. . . .* She remembered the tension between Felix and Liam, and she grimaced. *Well, God, You can work miracles, can't You?* She tried to recapture the quiet sense of God's presence that she had been feeling, but somehow it had evaporated. She climbed the stairs to the second floor, frowning.

"Is there a problem, Dorrie?" Margaret Truesdell stood at the top of the stairwell, looking down at her. "You look like a thundercloud."

Dorrie smiled sheepishly. "No. I was just thinking—" She broke off, unable to explain her thoughts to Margaret. She grabbed hold of an earlier thought. "I've been having some discipline problems with my class, I'm afraid. Alec MacIntyre gave me some suggestions about setting up some classroom rules. I'm planning to do that today."

Margaret walked with her down the hall. "Good. I'm sorry if I haven't been more available to you during these first weeks. Time always slips away from me during the fall—and frankly, I'd heard nothing but good about you, so I assumed you were doing fine on your own." She stopped outside Dorrie's classroom door and turned toward Dorrie. "I'm glad, though, that you've been getting advice from Alec. He's a very fine teacher, gifted, I might even say. I remember that as a new teacher, I found my friendships with more experienced teachers to be invaluable. So I've been glad to hear that you and Alec are getting to know each other."

"Yes. Yes, we are." Dorrie shifted her feet awkwardly. "Of course," she added, "I already knew Liam. He's been teaching longer than Alec." *Why did I have to bring Liam up?* She felt her face grow warm.

Margaret looked at her thoughtfully. "Yes," she said, "that's true. Liam has been teaching longer than Alec. But I—" She shook her head, and then she smiled. "Stop down to my office today after school, Dorrie. I'd like to hear how your new rules work out."

Dorrie agreed. She stood in the hall a moment longer after Margaret left. *Why do I feel so unsettled again, God? She didn't mention Liam, and yet I felt as though I had to bring him into the conversation, as though I had to defend him somehow against Alec MacIntyre. Why am I so silly sometimes?* She pushed the heavy hair back from her face, then opened the door of her classroom.

Inside, she was surprised to find Felix already seated at his desk, rather than inside his closet. He was hunched over a paper, his fingers tight on a drawing pencil, but he looked up when she opened the door. He pushed his glasses up his nose. "It's about time. I've been waiting for you."

Dorrie smiled. "I was talking to Mrs. Truesdell. Did you want something?"

Felix nodded. "Could you give me a Bible?"

ten

"Don't look so pleased," Felix said, shaking his head. "It's not like I asked you to help me convert or something. All I want is a Bible to read. I could ask my houseparents or Mr. MacIntyre, but I figured they'd get too excited. Make too big a deal out of it. So don't you go and do the same thing."

Dorrie walked over to her desk and opened a drawer. "I keep an extra Bible here. You can have it." She leaned to hand it to Felix. "Why did you want it?"

He shrugged. "Just curious. We hear so many sermons in this place, people quoting the Bible left and right. I thought I'd like to be able to check things out for myself. I don't like feeling like everyone has access to a source of possible information that I don't." He stuck his chin out and narrowed his eyes at Dorrie. "Notice I said *possible*. And who knows—maybe everyone's interpreting the whole thing all wrong. Maybe it really says something totally different when you look at the complete context. Know what I mean? I don't like to trust anyone's mind but my own."

Dorrie nodded. "Makes sense to me."

"It does?"

"Sure. No one can tell you what to believe. You have to figure that out for yourself." She turned away to open the curtains so he wouldn't see her smile.

He watched her for a moment. "You're not going to give

me some little tract with the twelve steps to salvation or something?"

Dorrie turned around and let him see her smile. "Nope."

Felix shook his head. "I'm surprised." He got up and put the Bible inside the closet with his other books. "Don't tell anyone. Not the other kids."

"How come?"

"They give me a hard enough time without them thinking I'm turning into a religious freak. I can just hear Kenny now."

Dorrie sat down at her desk. "You and Kenny are a lot alike in some ways, you know."

Felix made a face. "We're *nothing* alike. He's a big, stupid jock. All the other guys like him, he's good at all those stupid games Mr. Adams thinks are so important— and I'm little and smart, and none of the guys like me. When I have to be on someone's team, they all groan."

Dorrie nodded. "And I'm sure Kenny's just as envious of your reading and drawing abilities."

Felix scowled. "I'm not envious of him. Who wants to be a big, stupid jock?"

Dorrie shrugged. "See what I mean? You both insult the people you really envy—I think that's called sour grapes. You both like to be in control. You both have a hard time letting people get close to you—and you use your smart mouths to keep people at a distance. And you both have a hard time accepting authority. Don't you?"

Felix looked down at his drawing and erased a line. "Maybe," he said finally. He leaned over his drawing, his tongue between his teeth as he sketched the thick round lines of a hippopotamus. Dorrie leaned against her desk, watching him. He drew the bristles on the heavy jowls and then looked up at Dorrie. "Things were pretty bad in here on Friday with Kenny and the others, weren't they?"

Dorrie nodded.

"You really lost control, didn't you? Good thing for you that Mr. MacIntyre came along when he did."

Dorrie nodded again.

Felix looked down at his drawing. "I guess I started the whole thing, didn't I?"

Dorrie lifted her shoulders. "You started that particular incident. As Mr. MacIntyre would say, you were a whole lot less than appropriate. But it was coming anyway. Something like it would have happened eventually, whether you started it or not."

"So are you going to let us get away with stuff like that?"

She shook her head.

"Are you going to quit?"

"Nope."

"What are you going to do?"

Dorrie smiled. "Wait and see."

Felix squinted his eyes at her. "I bet you don't know how to be mean. Not mean enough to control us. Unless you've been taking lessons from your precious Mr. Adams. He's plenty mean."

Dorrie opened her mouth and then closed it. She looked out the window. "Like I said, Felix, wait and see."

❧

At the end of the day, Dorrie closed her classroom door and went down the stairs to Margaret Truesdell's office. Margaret looked up and smiled when Dorrie came through the door.

"How did it go?"

Dorrie looked around Margaret's office. It was

decorated in shades of green, and after her noisy class-room, it seemed to Dorrie as peaceful as a forest. She noticed the threadbare velvet curtains that hung at the windows, the worn velvet chairs that circled Margaret's desk; she sighed. "All right. Nothing miraculous." She smiled ruefully. "I guess I was imagining myself transformed overnight into the perfect teacher. But the atmosphere in my classroom has definitely changed. The kids weren't too happy about it—but I keep telling myself that doesn't matter. I think I'm starting to see the light at the end of the tunnel—or something. I guess what I mean is that at least I know what I'm working toward in my classroom—instead of just wandering aimlessly the way I'd been doing." She dropped into the chair that Margaret pushed toward her. "I never knew teaching would be so hard."

Margaret's gray eyes crinkled. "I've stood in the hall-way and observed you several times while you were teaching, Dorrie. You're a natural at it. You just need to get your stride, find your own personal rhythms. Once you do, you'll find you can relax more. But I do agree that teaching can be very difficult, especially if we're emotionally involved with something else. Teaching these particular students seems to demand a sort of emotional concentration."

Dorrie thought of the many times she had been distracted from her class by thoughts of Liam, sometimes even when she was in the midst of teaching. She nodded slowly.

Margaret leaned toward Dorrie and touched her arm. "I thank God that you came to us, Dorrie. Be patient with yourself while you grow. I know God is using you."

ë

"I thought you had to work tonight," Dorrie said to Clem

when she came through the door and found her friend curled up on the sofa.

Clem blew her nose and pulled a quilt around her shoulders. "I was supposed to. But I think I'm coming down with something. The doctor sent me home—said he didn't want me sneezing on all his patients." She wiped her nose again and shivered.

"You sound terrible. Can I get you something?"

Clem shook her head.

"How about some tea?"

Clem smiled weakly. "I don't know why you want to be nice to me when I've been so hard to live with lately."

Dorrie filled the kettle with water. She smiled over her shoulder at Clem. "Because I love you."

Clem's blue eyes glittered with tears. Dorrie put down the tea kettle and went to kneel beside her on the sofa. "Oh, Dorrie," Clem said, leaning her head against Dorrie's shoulder, "I've been feeling so awful inside. So hard. And scared. I know that can't be right. If I was really following God about not marrying Mason, don't you think I'd feel a sense of peace about it?"

Dorrie nodded.

"Well, I don't. I feel awful. Cold and lonely, like everyone I'm close to is getting further and further away. You, Gram and Grandpop, Mason—" She rubbed her eyes with her fists, and Dorrie thought she looked like an unhappy ten-year-old. "I just don't know what to do. I know I love him, Dorrie. But I *can't* marry him."

Dorrie stroked Clem's rumpled curls. "It's okay," she said gently. "The people who love you haven't gone anywhere—we're all still right here. We can wait while you figure things out. But probably tonight when you feel so sick isn't the right time to be doing any serious thinking. Just rest." Dorrie smiled, and then she repeated Margaret Truesdell's words to her, "Be patient with yourself while you grow." Clem sighed and blew her nose, and Dorrie got up and put the kettle on the stove.

While she waited for the water to boil, she told Clem about her day at school. "I guess I thought the kids would be as excited about making these rules as I was. They weren't." She shook her head. "They're so good at emotional blackmail—you do what I want, and I'll be your friend. At least now, I can see what they're doing—thanks to Alec." She poured the hot water over the tea bag and handed the steaming cup to Clem.

"Mmmm." As she drank, Clem smiled her thanks over the cup's rim. "So you admit that Alec's not such a bad guy after all?"

Dorrie shrugged her shoulders. "I admit he's a very good teacher."

"Better than Liam?"

Dorrie's lips tightened. "Liam's having some problems right now with his approach to teaching. That has nothing to do with how I feel about him."

"I understand," Clem said mildly. She sipped her tea in silence while Dorrie began to make supper.

৵

By the end of the week, Clem's cold was even worse. She huddled on the sofa, shivering and sweating by turns, the box of tissues tucked next to her. "I think you have the flu," Dorrie said when she came home from work Friday. She touched Clem's hot head, then went to the refrigerator and poured her a glass of orange juice.

"Thank you, Nurse Carpenter," Clem murmured as she

took the glass of juice. "How was work today?"

Dorrie smiled. "Better. Lots better. Things are really starting to settle down. There's a feeling of order to the classroom—and we all seem so much more relaxed. Like we're not all trying to prove something anymore, myself included. For the first time, I feel I can actually concentrate on teaching instead of trying to tiptoe around potential disasters the way I was doing. They were even quiet while I read to them this morning. And during their free time, I found Polly and Lamar in the reading corner—and they were actually reading."

She sighed and settled down in one of the big chairs. "Alec and I are going to have a 'store' together—things the kids can 'buy' with the points they earn for appropriate behavior. And next week, whoever has enough points can exchange them for a trip to the roller skating rink. Margaret has approved a bus to take Alec's and my classes."

Clem set the empty glass on the floor beside her. She coughed and pushed her limp curls away from her face. "Sounds good," she said listlessly, and then frowned, as though she were making an effort to concentrate. "A roller skating rink doesn't sound like something your friend Felix will enjoy, though."

Dorrie grinned. "No. Alec and I thought of that. So there will be another after-school trip offered the next day—this one to the art gallery. I'm pretty sure Felix will be the only one interested in that excursion." She stretched her long legs out in front of her, then kicked off her shoes. "I'm looking forward to having some time with Felix. I love all the kids, I really do, but there's something about Felix. I keep wishing I could bring him home and keep him."

The phone rang, and Dorrie leapt to answer it. During the week, she had been concentrating so hard on her students that she had barely thought of Liam. On the way home from work, though, she had wondered if she would hear from him over the weekend, and all the while she had been talking with Clem, part of her had been listening for the phone. Her heart pounded now as she picked up the receiver. "Hello?"

"Hi, Dorrie."

Dorrie let out the breath she had been holding. "Hi, Liam." She smiled.

"I know this is last minute again, but every time I've tried to talk to you at school, you seem to be busy with Alec MacIntyre."

"Just school stuff," Dorrie said quickly. "We've been working on a joint behavior management program for our two classes."

"Oh. Well, what I wanted to ask—are you busy tonight? I'd really like to see you."

"I'm not busy—" Dorrie started to say, and then she looked at Clem. "I'm not busy," she repeated, "but your sister is pretty sick. I think she has the flu. I hate to leave her after she's been here alone all day."

Clem made a face and waved her hand at Dorrie. "Go on," she whispered. "I'll be fine."

"Poor Clemmie." Liam hesitated. "I know. Ask her if she wants to go over to Gram's house. That's where she belongs if she's sick. She can lie in bed and be pampered and eat Gram's chicken soup. Gram will love it, and so will Clem. We could drop her over there, and then you and I could go out somewhere."

"Hold on," Dorrie answered. "I'll see what she says."

☙

"The house is going to seem empty," Dorrie said as she packed a bag for Clem. "I'm going to miss you."

"I don't know why," Clem sniffed. "I've been such a wretch."

Dorrie laughed. "You *are* sick, Clemmie, when you start sounding so pathetic." She looked out the window. "Here's Liam now. Think you can manage to walk out to the car?"

"I'm not an invalid," Clem said as she tottered toward the door. She leaned against the wall and shut her eyes. "But maybe it would be good for Liam to have to help me out to the car." She took a deep breath and opened her eyes. "You know, teach him to be more sensitive and empathetic. You just go out and tell him his little sister needs him."

Liam's smile was crooked when Dorrie repeated Clem's message. "I bet," he said, but he came out the door a moment later carrying Clem in his arms.

"I can walk," she insisted. "I just wanted to lean on you a little."

"Shut up, Clem," he said. "You weigh about as much as that old cat of Gram's. Besides, I used to carry you around all the time when you were little." He grinned as he put his sister in the truck and tucked a blanket around her. "Don't you remember?"

"Vaguely." Clem moved to the middle of the seat so that Dorrie could climb in beside her. "That was a long time ago."

Liam started the engine. "Before Mom and Dad died."

Dorrie saw Clem's small hands clutch the blanket tighter to her. "Yes."

Liam backed the truck out of their driveway. "You talked

to Mason lately, Clem?" he asked as he pulled out onto the dirt road.

"No."

"I didn't think so. I gave him a call before I came over here. Told him you were sick."

Dorrie saw Clem's head turn toward Liam. "Why ever would you go and do a thing like that?"

"I don't know. I guess I thought he'd want to know. So he can pray for you."

"Right." Clem's voice was dry. Her fingers tightened and loosened, tightened and loosened on the blanket. "You know," she said after a moment, "that's really not like you, Liam. If nothing else, you usually mind your own business."

"Usually." Liam's voice was mild. "I guess you could say I'm concerned about you, Clem."

Clem snorted.

"Well, I am. You seem pretty serious about breaking up with Mason. And that would be a really stupid thing to do."

"Yeah?" Clem's voice was tight.

"Yeah. You two are obviously right for each other. I'd hate to see you throw that away just because you're scared."

Clem's hands jerked tight into fists. "What do you know, Liam?"

Liam drove silently for a moment. "I know," he said at last, "that you're scared. I know that it's because of Mom and Dad. I guess—oh, I don't know. I guess you probably think that if you dare get married and be happy, then something will happen to Mason."

"How dare you, Liam," Clem said in a small, hard voice, "how dare you try to analyze me, when—when—" Dorrie heard her swallow hard, as though she were keeping back her words by sheer will power.

"I know," Liam said quietly, "I know. But maybe that's why I understand." He pulled into the Adams' driveway. "Look, Clem, I know you're sick, and this probably isn't the best time. But I know Mason is going to try to see you tomorrow, and I'd hate to have you turn him away. He's been accepted by the mission board—and one day he may not come back to you again." He turned off the motor, and Dorrie felt him slide his arm around Clem's shoulders. "Believe it or not, Clemmie," he said softly, "I love you." He got out of the truck, then reached back for Clem.

Dorrie followed them inside. She waited while Gram and Grandpop fussed over Clem and then bundled her upstairs to bed. "Get better," she told her friend. She looked down at Clem's small, pale face and saw the sheen of tears in her heavy eyes. "Don't worry about anything; don't think. Just rest. We all love you. I'll see you soon." She closed the bedroom door softly behind her.

Downstairs, Gram pressed her lips together and shook her head. "She hasn't been sleeping well ever since this thing with Mason. I could tell from her eyes. She looked the same way when something was troubling her when she was a child—and then she'd end up sick."

Grandpop put his hand on Gram's shoulder. "Well, she'll get the rest she needs now, with you to coddle her."

"I hope so." Gram shook her head again. "But I can't make her mind rest easy."

"No." Grandpop smiled. "But our Lord can."

Liam cleared his throat. "Dorrie and I are going to get going now."

Grandpop turned his smile on them. "Stay a while.

There's an old John Wayne movie on. Remember how you used to love them when you were a kid, Liam? Gram was just going to make popcorn."

Liam smiled, but shook his head. "Another time, Grandpop. Dorrie and I are going to go out to eat now."

Gram looked from Liam to Dorrie. "Have a good time," she said, her eyes resting thoughtfully on Dorrie's face. Dorrie felt herself flush, as though Gram could read her heart better than she could herself. Gram smiled. "We'll see you Sunday, children."

❧

They went to a dim Italian restaurant, nearly empty because of the late hour. Liam said very little while he ate. Dorrie watched his face, thinking of the love he had shown Clem. Again and again, she opened her mouth, about to say something about Clem and Mason, but each time she caught herself in time. Liam needed her to be quiet, she reminded herself. She tried to find the peaceful quietness she had experienced more and more during the past week, but her mind kept working busily, ticking off the many ways she loved Liam, as though she were keeping a score card.

After they had finished eating, he drove her back to her house. "Are you nervous about being alone?" he asked as they sat in the driveway.

Dorrie shook her head. "Not really."

"Want me to come in with you?"

Dorrie looked at him. "For a minute. I could make coffee."

Inside, Liam watched her while she made the coffee. The silence between them made Dorrie uneasy, but she forced herself to ignore it. She smiled at him while the coffee maker began its sighing and dripping. He smiled back.

"You look pretty tonight, little Dorrie."

"Thanks." *Not exactly a conversation opener*, she thought. The coffee finished brewing, and she poured them each a cup.

Liam took his cup and came to stand beside her where she leaned against the kitchen counter. She could feel his warmth very close, his shoulder brushing hers, but she felt tense and on edge. She looked into his face, and at last she could stand the silence no longer. "You were wonderful with Clem," she said softly.

His mouth twisted. "She wasn't exactly receptive to what I had to say. Not that I blame her."

"She's just so sick right now. But I know she'll appreciate what you said when she feels better."

Liam shrugged.

"I never thought before about what you said," Dorrie continued, "about her being afraid to marry Mason because of what happened to your parents. But it makes sense."

Liam sipped his coffee.

"I mean," Dorrie said, "the death of your parents at such a young age had to affect her psychologically. Both of you." She looked again into his face.

He smiled. Then he reached and took the coffee cup from her hand and set it on the counter behind them. "Shh, Dorrie," he said and pulled her into his arms.

Dorrie stood with her face against his beard, feeling awkward and breathless. After a moment, he turned his head and his lips touched hers, gently first and then more deeply.

"Oh, Liam," Dorrie said when at last they drew apart, "I love you so much."

eleven

Liam smiled and drew her close again. "I love you too, little Dorrie," he whispered as his lips found hers once more.

His kisses grew longer and deeper. At last, Dorrie pushed him away. "You'd better go," she said breathlessly.

"I suppose." His lips curved, while his hand moved up and down her back. "Can I come over tomorrow?"

She nodded. "Maybe we could go for a walk," she said shyly.

"Whatever you want." He pulled her tight against him one more time, and then he said good night.

For a long time after he left, Dorrie stood by the kitchen counter, surrounded by the quiet house. "Liam loves me," she said out loud. "Did you hear that? He said he loves me."

She threw the cold coffee down the drain and rinsed out their cups. Then she got ready for bed, wishing Clem were there to share her happiness. *She wouldn't be happy for me, though*, she reminded herself. *She'd be full of gloom and worry, saying all sorts of negative things about Liam. Better that she's gone tonight so I can enjoy this moment without her nagging.*

She lay in bed staring up at the dark ceiling, going over and over Liam's words, remembering his kisses. *I am happier than I have ever been*, she told herself. The house creaked quietly as it settled for the night; outside an owl hooted. Everything else was still, but in her mind, Dorrie thought she heard a whisper, *Who are you trying to convince?* She rolled over restlessly. After a long time, she slept.

≥≥

"Liam loves me," she said out loud as soon as she opened her eyes the next morning. Somehow, she still couldn't believe that last night had really happened. If Liam loved her, wouldn't she be nearly flying with joy?

She got up and showered. Remembering that he had said he would come over today, she dressed carefully and put on makeup. When she was done, she looked at her reflection thoughtfully. "Maybe you're scared to believe your good fortune," she said. "Maybe you're a little like Clem, afraid to believe that something so good can be true."

She made her bed and picked up her laundry, then moved around the house aimlessly, wiping the already clean table, plumping the patchwork pillows. "I should do some school work," she said and sat down on the sofa. She picked up her plan book, then put it down. She leafed through some of her students' writing, trying to concentrate.

When the knock came at the door, she jumped to her feet. "Oh, Liam—" She swung open the door.

Alec MacIntyre stood on her doorstep, his head ducked to look through the doorway. "Oh, it's you," Dorrie blurted. She stepped back to let him in.

"Were you expecting someone else?" He glanced around the room. "Where's Clem?"

"She has the flu," Dorrie answered. "Liam and I took her to their grandparents' last night."

"Oh." Alec looked at her thoughtfully. "That must have been where you were when I called." He shifted his weight awkwardly; when he looked down, Dorrie found herself noticing the way his lashes lay in a dark fringe against his cheeks.

"Did you want something?" she asked him.

He shrugged his wide shoulders. "Some friends of mine are cleaning out their attic. The kids are off to college now, and there's a bunch of old toys up there. They said we could take anything we wanted for our classroom 'store.'" He glanced at her, then picked up a pillow and turned it round and round in his big hands. "I was just wondering if you wanted to come with me to help sort through the stuff."

"I'd like to." She was surprised to find she meant her words. *I'm excited about working on the store, that's all.* She yawned, sleepy after lying awake the night before; she looked at Alec's bulky sweater and wished she could lean her head, just for a moment, against his chest. *I didn't get enough sleep last night. Either that or I'm losing my mind.* She shook her head firmly. "I can't today, Alec. I'd like to, but I can't."

He looked into her face. "Are you okay? You've got circles under your eyes. And you seem a little—I don't know—different. Soft around the edges or something." He frowned. "Maybe you're coming down with the flu too."

Dorrie shook her head again. "I'm fine." She had a sudden panicky feeling that Liam would come through the door at any minute. *What would be so bad about that?* she reminded herself. But she wanted Alec gone. She felt herself scowling, wishing suddenly she could take her hands and push him out the door. She imagined the way his sweater would feel beneath her fingers, and she found herself growing warm.

"You're flushed," Alec said, his eyes intent on her face.

"Maybe I *am* getting the flu," she said and turned away from him. "You'd better go before you catch it."

Alec smiled and shook his head. "You must be getting sick. You seem strange, Dorrie. Not like yourself."

I don't feel like myself. What is wrong with me? Liam loves me—and all I can think about is touching Alec MacIntyre. Her face burned even hotter.

She made herself smile. "No, no, really, I'm fine. Just busy." She pointed to her school books spread out on the sofa. "See? I promised myself I would get caught up on my paperwork today. You go and pick out whatever you think we can use. I trust your judgment."

"All right," he said at last, still staring at her. He put his fingers against her face. Dorrie flinched, and then stood very still, feeling as though she had been burned. His dark brows pulled together. "You're hot, Dorrie." His eyes met hers and suddenly he too flushed.

No, she wailed inside her head, *you can't be able to read my face that well. You can't know what I was thinking this time. I don't even know what I was thinking, so how can you?* She tore her gaze from his.

She saw his throat move, as though he had swallowed hard. "I'll call you later," he said in a strange quick voice, "to make sure you're okay. If you're feeling better and you get your work done, maybe you could come up later and help me organize the stuff." He let out his breath in a long sigh and dropped the pillow he still held back on the sofa. He smiled. "I'll even cook you supper, if you want."

Dorrie turned away from the hope in his eyes. "Maybe," she said. "I'll see."

ଶ

After he had left, she flung herself full-length on the sofa.

"What is wrong with me?" she cried to the quiet house. "I *know* I love Liam. I've loved him for years. I know he's the man God wants for me. I believe that. And now Liam finally loves me, too. We'll be married, and we'll have our own little house, and maybe someday Felix will live with us. . . ." She closed her eyes as though she could shut out the thought of Alec. "Maybe Satan is trying to tempt me away from God's plan for me. Maybe that's what's happening." She took long slow breaths. "But Alec MacIntyre?" Suddenly she giggled and put her hands over her face. "Oh, how can I be tempted by Alec MacIntyre? I don't even *like* him. And I love Liam so much."

She heard the sound of a motor outside in the driveway and jumped back to her feet. She ran her hand over her hair and then across her face, as though she could erase the warmth that still lingered in her skin. "Liam," she said as she opened the door for him, "I'm glad to see you."

He leaned toward her and kissed her lips. "Good morning, little Dorrie. Have you eaten yet?"

She shook her head.

"Want to go get some breakfast? I know this great little diner."

Over breakfast, Dorrie could stand the silence no longer. She found herself chattering about her class, about the new "store," about the planned trips to the skating rink and the art museum. Liam ate his scrambled eggs and said nothing.

When Dorrie at last fell silent, he grinned and lifted an eyebrow at her. "Being alone last night get to you, Dorrie? I don't think I've ever heard you talk so much."

Dorrie flushed and pressed her lips together. "I'm sorry."

"That's okay." He pushed back his plate and drew

patterns on his napkin with his fork, and then he shook his head. "But I have to tell you, I hate seeing you so influenced by Alec MacIntyre. I think his approach to the kids is all wrong. Giving them all these special treats—it's like you're bribing them to be good. They're such little manipulators, such users—they'll play the system for all it's worth and take all they can get. What they really need is a good firm hand. Come down on them hard if you have to, and let them know who's boss. A little healthy fear might teach them to have some respect."

Dorrie bit her lip. "I guess that's one approach," she said at last. "But even then I think you need to temper that firm hand with love."

Liam shrugged. Dorrie looked into his face, trying to read what he was feeling, but his blue eyes told her nothing. "Sometimes, Liam," she said slowly, "you seem so angry when I hear you talking with one of the kids. You —" She shook her head, determined to say no more.

He shrugged again and smiled. "Like you said, Dorrie," he said lightly, "we all have our own approach." He picked up the bill and pushed back his chair. "Let's not ruin a beautiful day by talking about the monsters."

He drove her back to her house, and they stood together by his truck, looking up at the blue sky that shone through the russet oak leaves. "What a wonderful day," Dorrie said.

He moved closer to her, so close that his breath stirred the loose hairs around her face. "Let's go inside," he murmured.

She looked quickly into his face, and then took a step away from him. "It's too beautiful to be inside," she said and grabbed his hand. "Let's go for a walk."

They walked down to the river hand in hand. *I must be*

dreaming, Dorrie thought. *This is one of my daydreams. This can't be real.* She looked sideways at Liam, noticing the way the sun caught the blue lights in his hair; he turned toward her and smiled, and his blue eyes were as clear and bright as the sky above their heads. She shook her head, as though to clear her mind. *Why don't I feel happier?*

At the fallen log, they sat down. Liam slid his arm around Dorrie's shoulders and pulled her against him. She closed her eyes, concentrating on the feel of him, the smell of him, but she found herself remembering instead the two times she had seen Alec here by the river.

In the sunlight, your hair looks just like a flame. Isn't that what he had said? She shook her head. *No, I will not think of Alec MacIntyre. I love Liam.* She turned her head and let her lips meet his.

The sound of a stick snapping made her jump and pull away. She opened her eyes. Alec MacIntyre stood below them on the river bank, looking up at them. His eyes were blank, his face as hard as though it were carved of stone.

twelve

"I'm sorry," Alec said stiffly. "I didn't mean to interrupt." He looked over their heads at the browning goldenrod behind them. "I called you on the phone." His eyes met Dorrie's quickly, then went back to the goldenrod. "When you didn't answer, I thought you might be down here." His mouth twisted. "Guess I was right."

"Alec—" Dorrie couldn't think of what to say.

He lifted his shoulders. "Sorry I bothered you." His hands in his pockets, he turned away. Dorrie frowned and watched him make his way through the trees until he disappeared.

"He likes you." Liam's voice was oddly gentle. "More than likes you."

Dorrie shook her head. She met Liam's eyes, but she couldn't read the expression she saw there.

Liam looked out over the river. "Actually, you know, you and he would look good together. You probably have a lot in common."

Dorrie grabbed Liam's hand and shook her head. He smiled faintly. "You look scared, little Dorrie."

She looked down at his long slim fingers, and then she took a deep breath. "It's *you* I love, Liam." She leaned toward him, waiting for his lips to claim hers.

❧

Liam picked her up for church the next day. Sitting beside him on the pew, she listened to his tenor voice singing the hymns, then watched the sure way he turned the pages of

125

his Bible. He glanced at her and smiled; she returned his smile and never once let her eyes stray across the church to where she knew Alec MacIntyre sat.

After the service, Gram Adams waited for them in the vestibule. "Come to dinner," she said. "Clem's lonely for some company." She turned as Alec came out the door. "You, too, Alec. Won't you have dinner with us?"

"No," he said. "I'm afraid I can't." He did not look at Dorrie. "Thank you for the invitation." He hurried away.

Gram watched him, two lines between her silver brows. She turned back to Dorrie and Liam, and her eyes fell on Liam's hand where it rested on Dorrie's shoulder. The lines between her brows grew deeper.

"We'd love to come," Liam said. "Right, Dorrie?"

She nodded, but she found she couldn't meet Gram's blue eyes.

After dinner, Dorrie went upstairs to spend some time with Clem. "How are you feeling?"

Clem smiled, but her cheeks were still pale. "A little better. I've been missing you—but it seems good to be back in the snug little bed I grew up in. Gram and Grandpop make me feel so safe."

Dorrie settled on the bed beside her. "Did Mason come over yesterday?"

Clem nodded. "But Gram wouldn't let him see me. Bless her. She said I needed to rest—physically and emotionally—before I try to make any more decisions." Clem sighed. "What a relief. I just don't feel up to facing him yet. I'm starting to have doubts about breaking up with him—and yet I still can't say I'll marry him. I just can't." Her hands clenched tight on the blanket.

"Don't think about it right now," Dorrie soothed. "Give

yourself time to heal."

Clem's hands loosened. After a moment, she sighed and fell back against the pillow. "What about you? How was your date with Liam?"

"Good." Dorrie picked a loose thread off the coverlet. "We had a nice time." She felt Clem's eyes on her, and she tried to say more, but the words stuck in her throat.

"You look awfully subdued," Clem said at last. "Did something happen?"

Dorrie hesitated. "He said he loves me." She held her breath, waiting for Clem's reaction.

"Do you believe him?" Clem's voice was mild, as though she were merely curious.

"I don't know." Dorrie met her friend's eyes. She took a deep breath. "I guess that's what's bothering me. Here I've wanted him to love me for so long, and now all of a sudden he says he does. It seems too good to be true."

Clem touched Dorrie's hand. "Just be careful, Dorrie."

❧

Dorrie felt better, though, after she had talked to Clem. *After all the things Clem's told me about Liam and women, it's no wonder I feel a little scared*, she told herself that night as she got ready for bed. *That's what's been bothering me, I know it is. It will just take a little time, time for me to know I can really trust him. Right, God?* Suddenly exhausted, she hurried into bed without waiting for an answer.

At school that week, Liam stopped by her classroom at least once a day. His blue eyes would smile into hers, and he would touch her hair or steal a quick kiss. On Tuesday and Wednesday, he ate lunch with her, and Dorrie found herself beginning to accept that he really did love her. She smiled and pushed the thought of Alec MacIntyre far to the back of her mind.

She was dreading, though, the trips with Alec and their classes to the skating rink and art museum. She had managed to avoid Alec all week, ducking into her room whenever she heard his voice in the hall. By Thursday, the day of the afterschool outing, she felt sick to her stomach with nervousness. *How can we be comfortable together professionally after what happened?*

To her surprise, though, he acted as though nothing had happened at all. He laughed with the kids and smiled easily at Dorrie as they circled round and round the rink on their skates. With a feeling that felt strangely like disappointment, she decided she had imagined that he was hurt by seeing her with Liam. *I must have imagined that he was attracted to me.* Hesitantly, she returned his smile. She let out her breath in a long sigh.

The next day, he met her at her room for their trip with Felix to the art museum. All of his own students had chosen the trip to the roller skate rink rather than this one, but to their surprise, Lamar had asked to go to the museum. The two boys sat on their desks, waiting for Alec and Dorrie.

"Think we can all fit in my car?" Alec asked.

Felix made a face. "I'm not riding in the back with all those cat hairs."

Alec grinned. "I thought you liked cats."

"I like *cats*. I don't like their unattached hair."

"Why don't we take my car?" Dorrie offered.

The two boys climbed in the back, while Alec sat in the front with her. "I'd sit in the back," he said, "but I don't think there'd be room for my legs."

Dorrie smiled and shook her head. She kept her eyes on the road ahead during the hour ride to the city art museum. Alec talked with the two boys, making them giggle with his stories.

"I was only thirteen, see," he said. "None of the other boys shaved yet. I felt like a freak. And here I was covered with little bits of light green toilet paper where I'd cut myself—and I mean covered with it. I looked like I was molding or something. And who should come to my house selling cookies but Allison Jenkins, the prettiest girl in my class. I took one look at her and—guess what I did?"

Dorrie smiled. She let their voices flow around her, and she found herself relaxing for the first time in what seemed like a long time. *It's because I'm beginning to believe that Liam really does love me*, she thought. *That's why I feel so happy.*

At the art museum, Felix was entranced. He stood so long in front of some works that eventually Lamar would grab him by the arm and drag him away.

"Come on, man, what's so fascinating?" Lamar asked. "It's just a picture of some flowers. It's not like it's a naked lady or anything."

Felix shook his head. "Look, look at the way he made this line. See? See the way it makes the flower look like it's moving, like the wind's blowing it. And look at the colors he used. That's something I'm not good at yet. I can get the lines. But I can't get the colors. Course, I don't have any oils. Maybe if I did. . . ." He let Lamar pull him to the next painting, still muttering under his breath.

Dorrie smiled. She looked at Alec, wanting to share her pleasure, but his eyes were on the painting. "Nice," he said and followed the two boys away from her.

"Can't I stay here while you go eat?" Felix begged when it was time for them to leave. "This is better than eating."

Alec ruffled his hair. "You do look like you're getting nourishment here that you need more than any Big Mac. But no, you can't stay by yourself. We'll bring you again, though."

Felix scowled. "Sure."

"I promise, Felix," Dorrie said quietly. "We'll get you here again."

But Felix scuffed his feet and would not look at her. At the fast food restaurant, he refused to eat his cheeseburger. He used a french fry to draw gremlin faces in his ketchup, and hung his head.

Alec talked easily to Lamar, making Dorrie realize how little she had gotten to know the other boy. She listened to them, sipping her soda, while she watched Felix out of the corner of her eye.

Suddenly, he raised his head and stared at her. "So," he said, "looks like I lost my bet."

"What do you mean?" Too late, Dorrie caught the quick shake of Alec's head.

Felix smiled, but his eyes behind their glasses were flat. "You and Mr. Adams. I put my money on Mr. MacIntyre, but it looks like he lost."

Lamar looked from Dorrie to Alec. "You dating Mr. Adams, Miss Carpenter?" he asked curiously.

"That's Miss Carpenter's business," Alec reminded quietly. "Now, who wants dessert?"

Dorrie found her eyes lingering on the strong bones of Alec's face. *He could look frightening*, she thought. *With that face, he could be some long-ago heathen warrior, swooping down to ravage and burn. And yet he's so gentle.*

She listened to him laughing with the two boys. *He's so good with them. If only Liam. . . .* She sighed. *Dear God, let Liam and Alec become friends. Liam could learn so much from Alec. . . .*

She drove the two boys back to the Home, and then Alec followed her home in his car. All the way, she felt his headlights in her rearview mirror, as though they were his eyes watching her. He honked his horn when she pulled into her driveway, and then she watched his lights disappear over the hill. She went into the empty house, feeling suddenly lonely.

❧

The next day Clem came home, still weak but with the roses back in her round cheeks. Dorrie tucked her in on the sofa.

"I'm so glad to have you home. This empty house was starting to drive me nuts."

Clem smiled. "No one to talk to, huh?"

Dorrie grinned. "You know me. I kept right on talking anyways. Nothing stops me. But I was starting to feel like a lunatic when I caught myself talking to a ladybug that was crawling on my window the other day."

Clem laughed. "What happened to this new, quiet Dorrie you were going to change into?"

Dorrie shrugged ruefully. "I guess I gave up on that for the time being. I can only handle so much at once." She looked at Clem. "Of course I still have faith that God will help me become the person Liam needs me to be."

"And vice versa?"

"What do you mean?"

"Is God going to change Liam into the person you need him to be too?"

Dorrie hesitated. "Well, isn't that the way it works? I mean, look at how perfectly Gram and Grandpop fit together, like two halves of a whole. They can't have started out that way, can they?"

Clem smiled. "No. You should hear Gram tell about some of their fights when they were first married. Of course, when people grow closer and closer, some of their rough edges have to get smoothed away. But I don't think who they really are changes, not the basic person inside."

Dorrie lifted her shoulders. "Well, I like the person that Liam is inside."

"So do I," Clem said. "I know you don't believe that, but I really do. I'm just not sure that person is the sort of man you need."

❧

All during the next weeks, while the dark red leaves turned brown and dropped off the oak trees, Dorrie felt Clem's eyes on her whenever she and Liam were together. He stopped at the house after school more and more, and every weekend he and Dorrie went out, then spent Sundays after church together.

Clem seemed quieter than usual, but Dorrie no longer felt she was shutting herself away from Dorrie the way she had before she got sick. She was still not seeing Mason, and Dorrie knew she spent long hours alone, praying for wisdom.

She no longer criticized Liam or questioned his relationship with Dorrie, but Dorrie knew she was watching them, listening to them talk. At last, one Sunday after they had all eaten dinner at the Adams', Clem watched Liam pull out of their driveway and then turned to Dorrie.

"You know," she said, "I think maybe he really does

love you."

Dorrie smiled. "I told you."

"I know, I know. But I couldn't help but watch for him to repeat the same old pattern of loving and leaving. But he hasn't. I don't think he's ever gone with a girl this long. Maybe he's finally serious."

"Of course he's serious." *After all, he and I are going to get married, aren't we? It's just a matter of time.* Dorrie looked at her friend's face and then threw up her hands in exasperation. "So why are you frowning now?"

Clem looked at her thoughtfully. "I think maybe Liam loves you. But I'm not sure you love him."

Dorrie laughed. "Don't be silly. Of course I love him."

❧

She was still smiling as she drove to work the next morning. *Oh God, You've worked everything out just like I dreamed You would. I knew Liam was the man for me. We'll smooth off our rough edges, and then we'll be so happy. . . .* His truck was in the parking lot, and she hurried into the school building, hoping to run into him in the hall.

She lingered by the main office, longing for him to appear, and then went up to her classroom. The room was empty, and so was Felix's closet. She sat at her desk, praying for the new day ahead of her, trying to quiet her mind and concentrate on her students, but she was too restless. After a moment, she jumped to her feet and ran down the stairs to the gym.

Usually, he came to see her in the morning, but today she would seek him out. *What if he feels like Clem, that I may not really love him? I should probably take the initiative more often. . . .* The light was on in his office, the door not quite shut. She smiled and pushed the door open. "Liam—"

Liam's arms were around a woman with long blond hair. Dorrie knew that a moment before, his mouth had been pressed to hers. The woman pulled away and looked at Dorrie; Dorrie saw she was the new third grade teacher who had come to the Home last week.

"I keep forgetting your name," Dorrie said, as though from a great distance. "But I'm sorry to interrupt." She did not look at Liam's face, but she saw his arms drop to his sides.

"I'm sorry, Dorrie," he said quietly. "I really did try."

thirteen

Dorrie turned toward Liam. She saw the clear blue blaze of his eyes against his dark hair and beard, the neat, slender bones, the long fingers that were never still. "I loved you," she whispered. She turned blindly away.

She found herself outside her classroom, with no memory of how she got there. Through the open door, she could see the light on in the closet. She turned away, knowing she could not face Felix now. Without thinking, she ran down the hallway, stumbling a little, to Alec's room.

When she burst through the door, he stood up and came around his desk toward her. "Dorrie—"

Tears streaming down her face, she flung herself at him. He stood very still for a second, and then his arms pulled her close. "Dorrie, what is it?"

She shook her head and pushed her face against his chest. She didn't want to talk or explain, didn't want to think or remember. She only wanted to stay here where she was safe and warm. Her sobs shook her entire body.

"Shh, sweetheart, shh." She felt his hand against her hair, stroking. He let her cry, saying nothing more while he held her tight.

After a long time, he drew back a little and tried to see into her face. "Dorrie?" He tipped her face up with his fingers. "What is it?"

Dorrie pulled away, suddenly embarrassed. "Liam. He was with— They were—" She gulped and stepped back.

"I'm sorry," she muttered. "I'd better get back to my classroom. The kids will be here any minute."

He kept his hands on her shoulders. She knew he was staring into her face, but she could not look at him. "No," he said finally. "I'll get your class and bring them down here with mine. We'll watch that science film we were going to show them tomorrow. You go for a walk. Get yourself calmed down."

She nodded, still not looking at him, and pulled away from his hands.

"Dorrie?"

She glanced at him quickly.

"I—I'll be praying for you."

She nodded and hurried away, afraid the students would catch her in the hall. She knew her makeup was ruined, her french braid mussed, and she did not feel strong enough yet to deal with their curiosity. She ducked into the women's room, then slipped out one of the school's back doors and ran across the soccer field into the woods.

The trees were nearly bare now, the wind cold through her sweater. She wrapped her arms around herself and leaned against a beech tree's smooth gray trunk. In the distance, she could hear the children's voices as they made their way from the cottages to the school building; close by, the only noise was the wind stirring the few dead leaves that lingered in the trees' limbs. Her tears had dried; she felt still and numb inside, as though her feelings had been frozen. Overhead, the sky was the pale chill gray of metal. Dorrie tipped back her head and looked up through the bare branches, remembering how blue the sky had been, how clear and warm, the day she and Liam had sat on the fallen log by the river. *As blue as Liam's eyes.* She shook her head and walked slowly back to the school building.

🙠

At the end of the day, she stuck her head in Alec's room. "Thank you for your help earlier. I really appreciate it."

He stood up and came toward her. She felt his eyes on her face, but she looked away and stared at Felix's mural of the solar system. "How did your day go?" he asked.

She lifted her shoulders. "All right. I was operating on autopilot, but the structure I've been building with the kids seemed firm enough to take that, at least for now." She smiled faintly. "I guess that's good, right?"

He nodded and came closer to her. "How are you?"

"I'm fine."

"Would you—would you like to talk?"

She shook her head. "Thanks, Alec. But I'm okay. I'm going to go home now."

🙠

Outside her house, though, she hesitated. Clem was already home. Somehow, Dorrie felt reluctant to face her. She took a breath and opened the door.

Clem was curled up reading in one of the chairs. "Hi," she said without looking up.

"Hi." Dorrie took off her jacket and hung it up. She went to the refrigerator and opened it. "Want me to get supper?"

"Sure." Clem's eyes were still on her book. "I took out a package of hamburg."

Dorrie chopped an onion. She mixed it together with the meat, added an egg and bread crumbs.

"How was your day?" Clem asked.

"All right." Dorrie took a loaf pan out of the cupboard. "Meat loaf sound okay?"

"Sounds fine. I think there's some potatoes left we could

bake." Clem closed her book and came to stand beside Dorrie by the kitchen counter. "I'll scrub them."

Dorrie pressed the meat into the pan. "No, I'll do it. You go sit down." She kept her eyes on her work.

Clem didn't move. "What's wrong, Dorrie?" she asked after a moment.

"What makes you think something is wrong?" Dorrie tried to make her voice light.

"You won't look at me. And your eyes look like you've been crying. What is it?" When Dorrie still didn't answer, Clem let the bag of potatoes tumble into the sink. "Is it Liam?"

"I guess you could say that." Dorrie picked up a potato and began to scrub it. "I found him kissing the new third grade teacher this morning." She carefully cut out the potato eyes. "Chances are he doesn't love me after all, don't you think?"

"Oh, Dorrie." Clem took the potato out of Dorrie's hands and put her arms around her. "Oh, Dorrie. I'm sorry."

"You're too short to hug me." Dorrie stepped away from Clem's arms. "I always feel like a giant next to you." She picked up another potato. "Aren't you going to say, I told you so?"

"No," said Clem, "I'm not." She touched Dorrie's arm. "I'm going to pray for you. And then I'm going to give my brother a piece of my mind." Her round eyes flashed.

Dorrie shook her head. "No, you're not. Not if you love me." She set the potato on the counter. "I think I'm going to go lie down for a little while. Call me when supper is ready."

She flung herself on her bed and lay with her face in her pillow. She found herself thinking about the next day's lessons, about the grocery shopping she and Clem needed to do, about anything except Liam. She picked her head up and made herself reach for the Bible she kept on the table beside her bed. Opening it at random, she stared blindly at the fourth chapter of Romans.

After a moment, however, words she had underlined registered in her brain. "God. . .calls into being that which does not exist. In hope against hope Abraham believed. . . he did not waver in unbelief, but grew strong in faith. . . ."

"Of course," Dorrie whispered. "Of course." She shut the Bible and went back to the kitchen.

"Feel better?" Clem asked.

Dorrie nodded.

While they ate, she felt Clem's eyes studying her. Dorrie only smiled.

❧

The next Sunday as they drove home from church together, Clem shook her head. "I don't understand this. You're too— serene. You go around with this little smile on your lips, looking like the Mona Lisa. Like you know a secret no one else does."

Dorrie's smile widened. "Maybe I do."

Clem turned her eyes away from the road to look at Dorrie, and then she shook her head again. "I don't get it. You've been infatuated with Liam for years. You finally see him in his true colors—and you act as though nothing has happened. What's up?"

Dorrie hesitated. "I just believe that everything's going to be all right," she said at last.

"Well, of course, it is. But I'm surprised that you've been able to see that so easily. I'm glad of course, but—" Clem looked away from the road again, her eyes narrowed.

"Wait a minute. You don't *still* think Liam is the man for you, do you?" She pulled over to the side of the road and turned so she could see into Dorrie's face. "No. You do." She rested her elbow on the steering wheel and put her forehead in her palm. "I don't believe it."

They sat in silence for a moment. "Listen, Clem," Dorrie said finally, "isn't that what faith is all about? Believing something despite the odds against it? So Liam isn't ready yet to make a serious commitment. That doesn't mean he never will be. The Holy Spirit is constantly at work in our hearts. You know that."

Clem pressed her lips together. She turned the key in the ignition, then swung the car out onto the road, heading back in the direction they had come.

"Where are we going?" Dorrie asked.

"To my grandparents'."

"I thought you didn't want to go for dinner today." Dorrie shifted uneasily in her seat. "What made you change your mind?"

Clem looked straight ahead. "Once Liam knew we weren't going to be there, I heard him tell Gram he'd be over. I need to talk to him. And so do you."

She pulled into the Adams' driveway. "Come on."

"Clem, I don't think—" But Clem was already opening the front door. Slowly, Dorrie followed her inside.

"What a lovely surprise, girls," Gram said, coming from the kitchen. She wiped her wet hands on her apron and leaned to kiss them. "I was just making the salad. I'm so glad you changed your minds about coming. I'll just set a couple of extra plates and—"

"I don't think we're staying, Gram," Clem interrupted. "We need to talk to Liam."

Gram opened her mouth and then shut it. "I see," she said at last, her eyes on Dorrie's face. "Well, he's in the living room. I'll just call Grandpop into the kitchen." Her blue eyes crinkled. "I think I need his help cutting those vegetables."

"Thanks, Gram." Clem returned her grandmother's small smile, but Dorrie's lips felt too stiff to curve.

"Come on, Clem," she whispered. "I don't know what you think you're doing, but—"

"I'm changing the station, letting some new voices into that busy little mind of yours, Dorrie Carpenter. I think the volume's been up so high inside your head, playing the same station, the same song for so many years, that you can't hear anything else."

"What do you mean?" But Clem had already gone into the living room. Dorrie hung back in the hallway, staring at the shiny curve of the stair bannister. She heard Clem's voice and then Liam's answer, she heard Gram and Grandpop's murmur from the kitchen, and then she tiptoed to the front door and quietly let herself out.

She pulled her jacket tighter around her shoulders and hurried across the yard, no goal in her mind except to escape.

"What's up?" Liam called from behind her. "Hey, Dorrie. Clem says you need to talk to me."

She turned around slowly. She shook her head. "I don't need to talk to you. Not right now." She smiled shakily. "You know Clem. She just has an idea in her head."

He nodded and then crossed the distance between them. "About you catching me with Stacey, right?"

Dorrie watched a crow wheel down out of the sky and land on the picket fence that bordered Gram's garden.

Nothing grew there now, only a few dead tomato vines still clung to their wire frames, and even the sturdy broccoli plants looked brown and frozen. She could not answer Liam, could not even bring herself to look at him.

"Dorrie?"

"I don't want to do this," she whispered at last, her eyes suddenly burning.

He took a step closer to her. "Clem's right this time, Dorrie. We do need to talk. Come back inside where it's warmer."

Dorrie felt as though a wave that had been frozen at its crest suddenly broke and crashed over her head. She could not keep the tears from streaming out of her eyes. "You said you loved me!"

Liam cocked his head to one side. "No," he said thoughtfully, "I don't think I ever *said* that, did I? I generally try hard not to lie."

Dorrie listened to his words, and she felt as though her feet had been swept out from under her by that raging wave of water. She closed her eyes. "How could you?" she whispered. "You were just playing with me, weren't you?"

"No." Liam's voice was regretful. "This time I wanted to love you. I really did. I tried. It felt so good knowing you loved me. I wanted to convince myself I could change for you." She opened her eyes and saw him shake his head. "But I couldn't. I'm sorry, Dorrie."

"Why didn't you tell me? Why did you let me go on making a fool out of myself? Why—" She heard her voice climbing higher, and she shut her teeth hard. *God calls into being that which does not exist*, she told herself, trying to stem the flood of her emotions. The words seemed suddenly flimsy, though, and they were swept away by the tide of hurt and anger that was spilling out of her. She looked at Liam's narrow, handsome face, and she saw no shame or sorrow there, only a faint regret. "You should have told me," she said between her teeth. "You shouldn't have let me stumble on the truth like that."

"I suppose I should have talked to you." He shrugged. "I hated to hurt you, little Dorrie."

"Don't call me that." She wiped her hand across her eyes and glared at him. "You didn't want to hurt me? How do you think I felt when I walked in on you kissing another woman?"

Liam shrugged. "I thought I could let you down slowly, gently." He smiled wryly. "I have lots of practice at that. I hadn't planned on what happened the other morning with Stacey. I've seen her a couple of times, I admit, but nothing more than coffee and talk. But then she came down to my office, and she was so sweet—" He shrugged again. "I like women. I like it when they like me." Beneath his mustache, his lips quirked. "What else can I say?"

"You can say you're sorry." Clem's voice was hard. She had come across the yard without either Dorrie or Liam noticing, and she came even closer to Liam now, her cheeks bright red, her blue eyes blazing. She looked as though she would like to swing one of her small fists at her brother, and he stepped backward, laughing.

"Hey, Clem, easy now. The last time you came at me looking like that you were ten years old—and I ended up with a black eye. Aren't we all grown up now?"

"Apparently not. Apparently some people never grow up." Clem shook her head. "You make me sick. You stand there and admit that you use women—and you don't even have the grace to be ashamed of yourself."

Liam's brows pulled together, but his voice was still mild when he replied, "We can't all be saints, Clemmie." He turned toward the house and started back across the yard.

"Oh!" For a moment, words seemed to fail Clem. Then she ran after Liam and grabbed his shirt sleeve. "You're the one who pretends to be the saint, not me. All your self-righteous talk, as though you were Mr. Super-Christian. It wouldn't be so bad if you were just a creep. But you're a creep who pretends to be a saint. And you have the nerve to say you try to be honest."

"You must have been eavesdropping for quite some time, Clemmie dear." For the first time, Dorrie saw a hint of red above Liam's dark beard. "Nothing very Christian about listening to other people's private conversations, is there?"

"Oh, for goodness sake." Clem sighed. "I was standing right there in plain sight, that's hardly eavesdropping. And this isn't about who is worse, me or you, you know."

"No?" Liam raised his brows. "Then what is it about?"

"You!" Clem let go of his sleeve, but she grabbed the front of his shirt and shook him. "You've been doing the same thing ever since Mom and Dad died. Aren't you ever going to stop?"

Liam pried her fingers off his shirt. He took a step backward. "I don't know what you're talking about."

"I'm talking about the way you changed after they died. You wouldn't let me close any more, you wouldn't let anyone close. And you act as though you're a Christian, when I know you aren't."

"How nice it must be to be omniscient." Liam's cheeks were very red now, his blue eyes blazing as bright as Clem's. Dorrie watched him glare into Clem's eyes for a long moment, and then he sighed and looked away. "You're right, of course. But," his eyes swung back to Clem's face, "I wasn't stupid. I could see the way you got all the attention, all the loving sympathy from Gram and Grandpop. You were the little Christian, and they adored you. So I decided to play the same game."

Clem stared back at him. "And here you are," she said at last, her voice quiet now, "fifteen years later, still playing the same game. Only now you play it with women."

Liam shrugged and looked away. "I don't see how that's really any of your business, Clem."

"I thought the fact that you're my brother and I love you made it my business. But if I'm wrong," Clem's lips tightened, "then when you start playing your games with Dorrie, then it certainly becomes my business. Here she thinks you're going to marry her—"

"Clem!" wailed Dorrie.

Liam's eyes swung briefly to Dorrie. "I never said anything about marriage; I'm sure of that."

"Oh, I'm sure you didn't. You try so hard to be honest." Clem's lip curled. "But poor Dorrie has been in love with you for years. For years and years she's thought you were the man God wanted her to marry." Clem glanced at Dorrie. "I'm sorry, Dorrie. But like I said, it's time to turn the volume down on whatever it is you've been listening to all these years. The only way I know to do that is with a good loud blast of reality."

Liam's eyes were resting curiously on Dorrie. "Why would you think God wanted you to marry me?"

Dorrie could feel her face growing hotter. The heat spread down her neck to her entire body. She shrugged and turned away, unable to look at the cool distance in Liam's eyes.

"Because she's an optimist," Clem said. "She loved

you—and so she thought sure that God would give you to her. She literally believed the Bible verse about God being a good Father who gives what we ask for—you know, 'if a son shall ask for a loaf, will he give him a stone? Or if he shall ask for a fish, will he give him a serpent?' She didn't know that what she was asking God for actually *was* a serpent."

Dorrie turned back and saw Liam's face flush still darker, until his skin was the color of bricks. He looked like a stranger, she thought. "How nice," he said. "How nice to know what my little sister thinks of me." He leaned forward and put his face close to Clem's. "Talk about being self-righteous. Well, while we're quoting Bible verses, what about the one that says to get rid of the beam in your own eye before you start picking at the splinter in someone else's? You take it upon yourself to straighten me out, to straighten Dorrie out—and meanwhile, you're not half so perfect as everyone thinks."

"I never said I was perfect."

"No, but you act as though you think it. What else would give you the right to interfere with me and Dorrie? Little Clementine, God's messenger on earth. But you know what? I'm not fooled by you, anymore than you've been fooled by me."

"What do you mean?" Clem's voice was suddenly small. "I'm committed to Christ. I really am."

"Oh, I'm sure you are. But you don't trust God any more than I do, not really. You'd never make Dorrie's mistake, because you know all too well that God does give His children stones and snakes. Why else would He have let Mom and Dad die?"

Clem's eyes were swimming with tears. "God knew what

He was doing. He loves us. I trust Him."

"No, you don't. If you did, you'd marry Mason. But you know all too well what can happen. Maybe I'm not honest in my relationships with women—but you're not honest either, blaming God for your refusal to marry Mason." Liam's voice was no longer angry. He sighed. "You've decided never to put yourself in the position where God can do to you what He did to you when our parents died. I don't blame you. But admit, at least to yourself, that that's what you're doing."

Clem closed her eyes. "They were so happy. We were so happy. We had the perfect life." She opened her eyes. "Didn't we, Liam?"

He nodded. "Close enough."

Clem rubbed her eyes with her fists. "When they died," she whispered, "we lost it all. I thought we were paying the price for being so happy." She looked from Liam to Dorrie. "I didn't want to ever risk being that happy again." She bit her lip, holding back a sob. "The price is just too high."

Dorrie crossed the distance between them and put her arm around her friend. "Talk about listening to the same station for too many years," she said gently. "You were right—we all needed a blast of reality." She looked over Clem's head at Liam and then pushed Clem toward him.

Liam opened his arms and pulled Clem close. "I love you, little sister. I probably haven't told you that for a while. But I do. And you're wrong—we didn't lose everything when Mom and Dad died. Because we still had each other."

Clem looked up at him. "You were right," she gulped, "I've been a self-righteous little prig, worrying about the specks in everyone else's eyes, when all the time I had a chunk of wood the size of a log in my own. I must have been so obnoxious."

Liam smiled. "You were. But we still love you." He watched Clem's eyes fill up with tears again and shook his head. "I've had enough of this standing out in the cold while we bare our hearts to each other. I'm going inside where it's warm. Gram must have dinner ready by now."

But when they turned back toward the house, they saw Gram sitting on the step, a blue sweater pulled around her shoulders. "I'm sorry," she said, "but I thought that if I pled guilty right away, then maybe listening to you children wouldn't count as eavesdropping. Grandpop probably won't speak to me when we go inside, but I was just too curious about what was going on."

Clem laughed shakily and leaned to hug her grandmother. "We have no secrets from you anyway, Gram."

"How can we?" Liam muttered, but then he grinned at Gram.

She looked back at him soberly. "I never realized before that we had failed you so badly, Liam. When your parents died, Clem was still a child, and it seemed—I don't know—easier somehow to comfort her. You were an adolescent, all cool and prickly. I should have known enough to reach past your defenses to where you were hurting. But I didn't. Will you forgive me?"

Liam opened his mouth as though to deny his grandmother's words. Dorrie saw Gram's eyes, still as bright a blue as Liam's, rest steadily on Liam's face. "Don't worry about it, Gram," Liam said at last and turned away. "I'm going inside. You women can stand out here in the cold all day, nattering and blubbering, if you want to. I can see that if Grandpop and I don't get dinner on the table, we'll all starve."

Gram watched him go inside. "He's not ready to truly forgive me." She sighed, then turned back to Clem and Dorrie. "No matter how old I get, I still find it so difficult to leave things with the Lord. I have a few voices of my own inside my head, and I've paid too much attention to them over the years, just like you girls. Over and over, I have to remind myself of that verse in Isaiah thirty: 'In returning and rest shall ye be saved; in quietness and in confidence shall be your strength.' Right now, I have to turn down all the other noise in my heart and just wait upon the Lord."

❧

"I'm trying to wait upon You, God," Dorrie whispered as she drove to work the next morning. "But it's hard." She felt empty inside, hollow.

After leaving the Adams' house, she had been glad to go home and fall into bed. For once, she was glad that Clem went to bed so early, for she did not want to talk things over, did not even want to think. And this morning she was glad to be driving to work, glad that she had her class. She thought of Felix waiting in her classroom and smiled. "At least I still have him."

She parked her car and walked toward the school building. A small woman with short dark hair and wire-rimmed glasses was waiting on the step. "Can I help you?" Dorrie asked.

The woman turned to her, her forehead creased. "I want to talk to someone who's in charge. I'm Terri Jones. I've come to take my son Felix home."

fourteen

"She can't just take him home with her, can she?" Mrs. Jones was with Felix now, and Dorrie strode from one end of Margaret Truesdell's office to the other.

"Of course not." Margaret's gray eyes were calm, too calm, Dorrie thought. "But from what she says, the family court judge who placed Felix here has now decided that Mrs. Jones is ready and able to have Felix back in her home. We can't release him to his mother's custody until the necessary paperwork comes through the mail—but if his mother's right, then it's just a matter of time."

Margaret's delicate brows drew together, and she put a hand on Dorrie's shoulder. "This is hard for you, I know. These children need us to care for them, to put our own hearts on the line. The only problem with that is that sooner or later we get hurt."

Dorrie shook her head. "It's not fair. Felix was just starting to respond to me. He asked me for a Bible— He comes in early and we talk— I was so excited about—" She swallowed hard and shook her head again. "The judge is wrong. Felix is so special, so talented. He can't go back into that horrible environment."

Margaret poured a cup of spearmint tea and handed it to Dorrie. "Sit down and drink this. Your class will be ready for you soon, and you need to calm yourself."

Reluctantly, Dorrie sat on the edge of one of the shabby velvet chairs that clustered around Margaret's desk. She sipped the hot tea and took a long, deep breath, but her knees jumped and jiggled, and she longed for Margaret to tell her there was some action she could take to change things. "What can I do? There must be something we can do."

Margaret smiled and shook her head. "I'm afraid not. Mrs. Jones tells me she's been participating in an intensive counseling program. She has a new job, one that she likes and that pays better money. She insists that she's changed—and I must admit, she seems like a different, happier person. She's even taking a night class at the state college."

"That's nice for her." Dorrie's voice was cool. "But that doesn't mean that Felix will be any happier living with her than he was before."

Margaret wrapped her slender fingers around her own cup of tea. "I think it does mean he'll be happier, Dorrie. Felix comes by his intelligence honestly, you know. His mother is very smart—and she was frustrated by her previous low-paying job. When Felix came here, she was beaten down by the pressures of her life, unable to cope with the responsibilities of being a single parent with a dead end, monotonous job that didn't pay enough to meet their needs—and unfortunately, she was taking her frustrations out on Felix. Neither one of them were functioning well. But that doesn't mean they don't love each other or that they don't belong together."

Margaret took a swallow of her tea and smiled at Dorrie. "Mrs. Jones has apparently gotten some much needed help. In fact, I would call the new life I sense in her remarkable, miraculous perhaps. I'm sure you've been praying for Felix—and I suspect the change in his mother is the answer to those prayers."

"I have been praying for him. But I wasn't praying that —" Dorrie broke off and shut her lips tight, knowing her words would sound bitter and unloving.

Margaret's smile deepened. "I know, Dorrie. I don't always like the way God answers my prayers either. I have my own ideas about the way things should work out—and then I'm disconcerted by the way God works His will instead." She shook her head. "This business of quieting our hearts so that we're open to what God wants—it's not always easy."

She set her cup on her desk and leaned back. "But, Dorrie, if you love Felix, then I believe you have to accept that being with his mother is the best thing for him. Our students need to get out of their home situations, and that's why they come here—but most of the time, after they've had time to work on their problems and so have their parents, the best thing for them is to go back to the people they love. As hard as we work to make the Home a loving environment, we're just not the same as a family."

Dorrie stared down into the green tea and frowned. "So you believe the Home gives happy endings for these kids?"

Margaret sighed, and once again her brows knit together. "Most of these kids come from homes that are so scarred and damaged that no completely happy ending is possible. But I do believe the Home can open some windows that will let in flickerings of God's grace. I have to trust that somehow, someday that grace will bring healing, whether it's in the ways I imagine and long for or not." The lines between her eyebrows softened. "In the particular case of Felix Jones, I have great hope. And so should you."

She glanced at her watch and got to her feet. "Go on, Dorrie. Get up to your classroom. And don't let your hurt make you afraid to love." Her lips curved. "Christ loved us—and His love made Him vulnerable to hurt, even to the point of death. But look what life came from it!"

❧

"I'm going home pretty soon." Felix sat on his desk after the other students had left for the day. Dorrie glanced at him, trying to read his expression, but his dark hair hung over his glasses, and she could tell nothing from the straight line of his mouth.

"I heard." She turned to stack workbooks in a pile on the corner of her desk. "How do you feel about that?"

Felix snorted. "How do you think I feel? I'm glad. I can't wait to get out of this dump. This place drives me crazy."

Dorrie looked up at him. "I'll miss you," she said quietly.

He shrugged and turned away. "I'm going to clean out my closet," he said over his shoulder.

Dorrie watched him pack his art supplies and books neatly into a cardboard box. Her eyes blurred, and she went to stand by the window so he wouldn't see her tears. "I'll see you tomorrow," she said when he had finished.

"Maybe. If I'm not gone by then." He ran out the door before she could say anything more.

Dorrie sat down at her desk and put her head in her hands. *I don't understand, God. Everything I hope for turns to ashes. I know You alone are all that I truly need. But I'd thought—*

"How're you doing?"

Dorrie raised her head quickly. She rubbed her hand across her eyes and smiled. "Hi, Alec."

He came in and leaned against her desk. As usual, his physical presence overwhelmed her, his size and the warmth that seemed to radiate from his body, but today she found herself comforted rather than repulsed. She got to her feet, however, and crossed the room to the windows; if she didn't put some distance between them, she was afraid she would give in to her longing to reach out and touch him.

"Margaret tells me it's God's will for Felix to go back with his mother," she said, her eyes on the brown line of bare trees that edged the playing field behind the school. "I'm having a hard time accepting that."

"I don't blame you." His voice was quiet. She found herself comparing the deep huskiness to Liam's light tenor, and mentally shook herself. *The last thing I need is to imagine myself in love with someone new right now.* She heard him move and sensed he was standing close behind her now; she fought the urge to lean back against his warmth. *Dear Lord, what is wrong with me? How can I feel so attracted to Alec now, when I'm so upset about Felix, when I'm still so confused about Liam?*

"Margaret says his mother's changed," Dorrie said, forcing herself to ignore the excited messages her body was sending her because of Alec's nearness. She turned to look up into his face. "Do you think Felix will be all right?"

Alec shrugged. "I don't think his life will ever be perfect, Dorrie, if that's what you mean. He and his mother will always have to struggle." He stuck his hands in his pockets and lifted his shoulders again, his eyes fastened on her face. "I'm not happy about him leaving either. But I do think things will be better for him and his mother, at least for now. And I have faith that God will continue to follow Felix throughout his life."

He took a step closer to her. She lowered her eyes from his face and stared at the blue and green plaid of his shirt;

her hands curled into fists as she fought the urge to feel the soft flannel with her fingertips. He reached out a hand and slid his knuckles along the line of her jaw. She shivered and swallowed hard.

"How are you, Dorrie Carpenter?" he asked softly. "This has been a hard time for you, hasn't it?"

She nodded and smiled faintly, though she could not meet his eyes. "First Liam and now Felix." She shook her head. "Just a few weeks ago I felt as though life was falling into place so neatly. Now I feel as though someone took the pieces of my life and tossed them into the air. The pattern I thought was shaping up so nicely isn't there at all anymore."

Alec smiled. "Maybe you'll find there's a brand new pattern. Remember what I told you once about God liking to surprise us?"

Dorrie nodded. "You said God was like a jack-in-the-box." She met his eyes and grinned. "I didn't know what you were talking about. All I knew was that it made me feel uncomfortable—and that made me annoyed with you."

"Seemed like most everything I did annoyed you back then." He returned her grin, but she saw the watchfulness in his eyes, as though he feared that reaction from her again.

They looked away from each other and turned toward the windows. Dorrie looked out at the cold, gray sky, but she was very aware of the warm, quiet room around her and of Alec's presence beside her, his shoulder nearly touching hers.

"I feel so stupid about Liam," she said at last, her voice barely more than a whisper. She did not want to tell him this, but something in the quiet room seemed to draw the words from her mouth.

"Stupid? What do you mean?"

"Embarrassed, I guess. Like I made a fool of myself."

From the corner of her eye, she saw Alec shake his head. "We all make fools of ourselves sometimes." He moved, and she felt his shoulder brush hers. "I've been imagining you feeling hurt, heartbroken. But not embarrassed."

"I *was* hurt," she said slowly. "But then when I saw Liam again, it was the strangest thing. Like Paul when the scales fell from his eyes. I looked at Liam, and I realized that the man I had been in love with so long had only existed in my mind. I'd been infatuated with an imaginary person. I felt so silly."

She took a deep breath, trying to ignore the way the warmth of his shoulder was making her heart pound. "Now I keep remembering when Felix accused me of talking to an imaginary friend. When he'd overheard me praying, remember? And I wonder if maybe he was right. Maybe God's been a figment of my imagination, just like Liam was. Like maybe I thought my life was a story I could create all on my own, and God was just one more character in that story."

She moved away from him slightly and put her palms against the cold glass of the window. "That's what scares me the most. And now when Margaret and you tell me to have faith, that God will take care of Felix, I think, 'Of course, that's what would be nice to believe.' But it was nice to believe the fairy tale I'd made up about Liam, too." She looked over her shoulder at him. "How do I dare have faith in anything again?"

He was silent for a moment, his eyes focused beyond her face on the darkening sky outside the window. "Seems to me," he said at last, his voice slow and careful, "that in any relationship there are times when communication breaks down. Our selfishness gets in the way, and we hear what we want to hear, see what we want to see, instead of being truly in touch with the reality of the other person."

She waited for him to continue. When he didn't, she felt her old impatience with him for a moment. "So?" she asked at last.

His gaze focused on her face. "So that's what happened with you and God. You had a communication breakdown. When you realize that's been happening with another person, I don't think you walk away and say, 'I'll never talk to that person again.' Or, 'Because I misunderstood that person once, I'll never believe anything he says again.'"

The curve of his mouth was so tender that she looked away, afraid to believe what she was seeing. She realized she was behaving in almost the way he was describing, and she forced herself to look into his face again.

His smile widened. "God's not your imaginary friend, Dorrie. You may have been treating Him like one. That's why He had to leap out of the box you'd been putting Him in, confront you all over again with the boundlessness of His reality. But He's bigger than you thought, *more* real, not less. He's giving you the chance to grow in faith—you don't have to shrink back out of fear and embarrassment."

He put his hand toward her again, then dropped it before it reached her. "Believe me, I know how scary this is. Like the people who lived with Christ nearly two thousand years ago, we'd all like to put Christ somewhere small and confined, where He won't threaten the way we want our lives to go. Then we'd roll a stone in front of the opening, just like they did, and never realize that we're as guilty as they were of crucifying His life."

Dorrie felt a shiver of joy. "But He won't stay dead, will He?"

Alec shook his head. "Thank God for the Resurrection." He turned and leaned against the window sill, facing her now. "It's funny," he said. He opened his mouth as though about to say something more, then closed it again. The silence stretched between them, suddenly tense where before it had been peaceful.

"What's funny?" she prodded at last.

He shrugged, and she watched, fascinated, as the tips of his ears turned red. He cleared his throat. "I guess," he said at last, "that I've had my own communication break-down with God. Kind of along the same lines as you. Except," his hands gripped the window sill behind him until his knuckles whitened, then loosened, "I thought God wanted me to remain single all my life. You know in First Corinthians seven where Paul talks about how if you're single it's better to stay that way?"

"I guess." Dorrie smiled a little sheepishly. "I have to confess that it's not a passage I've paid a lot of attention to."

"Well, I never had either. But then a couple of years ago, I was dating this girl. We didn't have a whole lot in common, I suppose, but I'd been lonely and getting involved with her seemed like a good idea at first. But then she started wanting to change me. She'd come over to my house and start sorting through my books." He shook his head and grinned. "She even wanted me to get rid of Esther. She was pushing me for a more serious commitment—but one day when I was praying about our relationship, I opened up the Bible to First Corinthians seven, and I thought, 'That's it. God's calling me to be single.' I felt so relieved."

"You—" Dorrie hesitated, not certain what she wanted to say, "you don't think that's what God wants for you after all?" she finished at last.

Alec grimaced and shrugged. "I wish I knew. All I do know is that I was guilty of using the Bible as though it were a fortune cookie. Oh, I believe that God uses Scripture to speak to us. But I see now that I was using the Bible just to support what *I* was already thinking, instead of using it to search for God's thoughts."

Dorrie nodded. "I did that, too, with Liam. Even after what happened the other morning. I opened up to a verse and convinced myself that I would be like Abraham if I continued to have faith that Liam, against all odds, would one day marry me." Alec's dark eyes on her face made her flush. She shook her head. "I see now how silly I was being. But what made you decide you'd been wrong?"

She'd asked the question innocently, truly curious, but something in his face made her breath catch. She saw him suck in a deep breath of his own. "You," he said at last.

"Me?" She didn't understand.

He nodded and the high planes of his cheeks were now as red as his ears. "You." He looked past her, studying a map of the world she had hung on one wall. "At first, I thought it was just because you were so pretty. I'd been feeling lonely again and—" He shrugged. "I figured it was only human to feel attracted to someone now and then. I thought we could be friends and that would be enough." He smiled faintly and his eyes flickered toward her, then back to the map. "But you didn't want to be friends. And I couldn't get you out of my mind." His voice was very low. "You finally let me be your friend—and then I realized," his mouth twisted, "that I wanted to be much more than your friend. I don't know anymore what God wants for the future. I only know what I want."

Dorrie found it hard to take a breath. "Well," she said, trying to make her voice light, "I know now how confusing God's will can be."

Alec shook his head. "I said I don't know what God wants for the future. For now, I think I do know."

Dorrie looked out the window. The sky was nearly dark now; Clem would be wondering where she was, she thought absently. "What is it you think He wants?" she whispered at last, still not looking at his face.

He cupped her chin with his hand. "I think God wants me to love you, Dorrie Carpenter," he said. She stared at him, saw him take a breath and swallow hard. "I haven't wanted to. You were so obviously in love with Liam. You didn't even like me. The more I cared about you, the more it hurt." He shook his head. "And yet somehow, I felt more alive, more aware of God's presence in my life, than I had in a long time."

She bit her lip, not knowing what to say. His hand dropped from her face. "I'm sorry," he said. "I didn't mean to say all that. I don't want you to feel awkward around me. I truly do want to be your friend." He shook his head and pushed himself away from the window sill, as though ready to leave. "I'm sorry."

"No—" She put her hand against his chest to stop him. She looked up at him. "I—" She could not continue. He looked down at her, and for once she was grateful that he could read her face so well, that she would not need to find words for the emotions that suddenly threatened to overwhelm her.

"Dorrie?" Very slowly, his hands went to her shoulders

and drew her closer. Even more slowly, his mouth lowered to hers. She felt the warm gentleness of his lips and though her heart continued to pound, she sighed, as though at long last, after the months of turmoil and confusion, she could relax.

A knock at the door made them spring apart. "I'm so glad you're both still here," Margaret Truesdell said when Dorrie opened the door. "Felix Jones has run away."

fifteen

Dorrie stared at Margaret. "But why would he run away now? He sounded so excited about going home."

Margaret shrugged. "He knows what life was like at home before. Could be he's scared." She shook her head. "His mother's downstairs. When I told her this morning that we couldn't release Felix without the necessary paperwork, seems she drove directly to the judge's office and insisted she give her the papers. She brought them back to me this afternoon after classes were dismissed. Everything looked to be in order, but I called the judge just to double check. She confirmed that it was okay to send Felix home. I sent word over to Felix's houseparents, and Mrs. Jones and I talked a little more. When we were done, we walked over to Corinthians Cottage—and found that Felix had disappeared." Margaret sighed. "Mrs. Jones is pretty upset."

"He hasn't had time to go far," Alec said quietly. "Let's search the grounds."

❧

An hour later, they still had not found him. "He used to hitchhike sometimes," Terri Jones said. Her face was white and pinched. "If he got a ride with someone, he could be anywhere by now."

Alec and Dorrie exchanged looks. "We'll drive around town and look for him, Mrs. Jones," Alec told her. "Don't worry. We'll find him."

They took Alec's car and drove slowly up and down the

streets of the small town. "I'm scared," Dorrie said.

Alec reached over and put his hand on the back of her neck. "He's smart, remember? He won't do anything stupid."

"But he's only eleven years old."

"He's used to taking care of himself. Just keep praying."

Dear Lord, I know You're with Felix right now. She felt the warmth of Alec's hand against the back of her neck; she felt the assurance of God's love like a warmth that touched her heart. Slowly, she relaxed. She let out her breath in a long sigh.

"Do you think he would have gone to the art museum?" she asked Alec.

They drove the hour long trip into the city, but by the time they got there, the art museum was closed and dark. They parked the car anyway and walked around the building, peering into window wells and behind bushes. At last, they got back in the car and drove to a pay phone.

Dorrie waited while Alec called Margaret back at the Home. He came out of the phone booth and shook his head. "Still no sign of him. Margaret says they've called the police. Mrs. Jones has gone home in case he should show up there. Margaret says we should go home too."

When at last they reached the turn to their own road, Alec glanced at Dorrie. "Mind leaving your car at the Home overnight? I'll drive you to work tomorrow."

Dorrie nodded.

He pulled into her driveway. After a moment, he turned off the ignition and reached for Dorrie. "Come here a minute."

She slid closer to him, glad for his warmth.

"This isn't the right time to talk," Alec said. "I just wanted to make sure I didn't dream what happened earlier." He turned toward her and hesitated, then gently put his lips against hers. "Get some sleep," he whispered after a moment. "Felix is all right."

She nodded, then opened the car door. She started to swing her legs out, then turned toward Alec again, wanting to feel his warmth one more time. She, too, felt as though she were in some strange dream.

"Looks like I won my bet after all."

Dorrie leapt out of the car. "Felix!"

He was huddled on her doorstep, his arms wrapped around his knees. He shivered. "Where have you been? I've been waiting for you for hours." The light from the car's interior glinted on his glasses; his voice was cross.

"Felix." Dorrie grabbed him and hugged him tight.

"What's the big deal? You into hugging everybody today, or what?" She saw his grin. "I saw what you and Mr. MacIntyre were doing. So much for Mr. Adams, huh?"

Alec came around the car and looked down at Felix. "Do you know how worried we've been about you?"

Felix shrugged. Dorrie still had her arms around his shoulders, and though he scowled at her, she noticed he did not pull away. "Why did you run away?" she asked him. "Didn't you want to go home with your mother?"

"Of course I want to go home." He did pull away from her then. "I'm not stupid. I wasn't running away. I just wanted to see you before Mom and I took off. I was afraid if I asked her to bring me here, she wouldn't, so I caught a ride here by myself. How was I supposed to know you wouldn't turn up for hours. Off smooching with Mr. MacIntyre probably."

"We've been looking for you," Dorrie said. "All over.

We even drove into the city. They've called the police to help search for you. Your mother's worried sick."

Felix shook his head. "Oh, great. Like I need to be in trouble with the police before I even get back home." He shook his hair out of his eyes and looked up at Alec. "This won't mean they'll change their minds about letting me go home?"

Alec shook his head. "I don't think so. But maybe next time you might think about the consequences a little more before you decide to do something on your own." He reached out and messed Felix's hair. "So what was it you had to see Miss Carpenter about?"

Felix looked down at his sneakers. "I just wanted to say goodbye, I guess." He looked up at her quickly, then shrugged his backpack off his shoulders and reached inside. "And I have something for you."

He pulled out the Bible she had given him. She thought he was going to give it back to her, and she started to shake her head, but instead he pulled a square wrapped in a paper towel from between its pages. He handed it to her.

She unwrapped the paper towel and found a piece of thick drawing paper, covered with the intense jewel colors of markers. She held the paper toward the light from the car and saw a fantastic bird, each feather perfect, blood-red against the glow of a rising sun.

"It's a phoenix," Felix said. "You know, those mythical birds that die and then rise out of the ashes back to life." He pushed his glasses up his nose and looked up at Dorrie quickly. "I've been reading the Bible you gave me. I thought maybe a phoenix would be appropriate for a Christian."

Dorrie blinked the tears out of her eyes. "It's beautiful," she said. "Thank you. I think it's the best gift anyone ever gave me."

"Really?" Felix stared up into her face. "Then how come you're crying?"

"Oh, Felix!" Dorrie hugged him tight again. "I'm going to miss you so much."

Alec put his hand on her shoulder. "This doesn't have to be the last time we see Felix, you know. I seem to remember you made a promise to Felix about going to the art museum again. I think probably your mom wouldn't mind if we kept that promise, would she, Felix?"

Felix grinned and shook his head.

"But not if we don't let her know soon that you're all right. Mind if we come inside and use your phone, Miss Carpenter?"

❧

"I can't believe he was sitting out on our step all evening, and I never knew it," Clem said later that night. Alec and Dorrie had driven Felix back to the Home, where his relieved mother had been waiting. The last Dorrie had seen of him he had been turned toward his mother as they walked to their car, talking quickly, his face flushed and excited.

Dorrie sank down onto the sofa. "What a day!"

Clem looked at her. "Looks like it was a pretty good day for you and Alec."

Dorrie shook her head and grinned. "You don't miss much, do you?"

"Nope." Clem settled cross-legged in one of the deep chairs. "So—tell me what happened between you two."

"I'm not sure." Dorrie looked down at the picture Felix had given her. "I guess—I guess all the while I was so busy thinking about Liam, some hidden, quiet part of me was falling in love with Alec. I didn't want to accept it. I was so used to thinking that Liam was the man for me that it scared me to even think about Alec. The more attracted I felt to Alec, the more I had to insist that Liam was the one I loved. Does that make any sense?"

"Nope." Clem rested her chin in her hand and smiled at Dorrie. "But I understand. I've been just as silly about Mason."

"Have you talked to him yet?"

Clem nodded and her smile widened. "Today wasn't such a bad day for me either. Mason and I went for a long walk after work today."

"And?"

"And I told him how much I love him. And that no matter how scared I am, I want to marry him." She held out her left hand and Dorrie saw the gleam and glitter of a diamond ring. "Seems he had faith that I would finally say yes."

"Oh, Clem!" Dorrie leapt across the room and hugged her friend. "Congratulations! I'm so glad you worked things out."

"Me, too. Mason says he would have waited for me no matter how long I took. But I would have been pretty sorry if he'd left for the mission field without me, and I would have had to wait a couple of years before I could see him again." Clem smiled down at the solitaire. "Liam would probably hate to admit it—but God really used him when he confronted me yesterday."

Dorrie nodded. "It's funny," she said slowly. "I was so sure that God was going to give me this tidy, little happy ending with Liam and Felix, just because that's what I thought I wanted most. And you were so sure that God was going to give you a sad ending if you dared marry

Mason, just because that's what scared you most. But we were both doing the same thing." She sank down on the floor beside Clem's chair and looked up at her friend. "We were both listening to our own voices instead of God's. The story I was telling myself had God confused with a fairy godmother—and the story you were listening to had God cast as a frightening, punishing ogre."

She reached for Felix's drawing and smiled. "Felix accused me once of living in a fairy tale. Well, I guess he was right. And now I see that God's reality is so much better, so much bigger, and more wonderful than the fairy tale."

Gently, Dorrie touched the phoenix's burning colors. "For a while there, I felt as though everything I'd longed for had turned to ashes. And now—now that our hearts are finally quiet and open to God—look what life has risen from it all!"

૭ৡ

On a Saturday nearly a month later, Alec and Dorrie drove home together from a visit to the Jones' trailer. Alec pulled into Dorrie's driveway and turned to her. "Felix really liked the oil paints you gave him. They were the perfect gift."

"The expression on his face when he saw them—I think he was even more excited than he was when we took him back to the art museum. I'm glad his mother doesn't mind us seeing him."

Alec nodded. "I like Terri. I can see where Felix gets his quirky sense of humor. They both seem pretty happy—and did you notice that Bible you gave Felix was lying on the coffee table? I have a feeling that God's taking good care of Felix and his mom."

Dorrie smiled. She looked out the car window and

watched the snowflakes that floated down, drawing white lines along the branches of the oak trees.

After a moment, Alec reached out and took her hand in his. "You've been so quiet since we left the trailer court. What are you thinking about?"

Dorrie looked down at his long, wide hand intertwined with hers. She felt her face grow warm, but she lifted her gaze to his and answered honestly. "I was remembering the day when Felix left. When you and I were together in my classroom. You said you didn't know anymore what God wanted for the future—but that you knew what *you* wanted. I was wondering what you meant."

"Nosy, aren't you?" He grinned, but she saw his dark lashes lower, as though he were uncertain of her reaction. His thumb moved back and forth on her hand. "I meant," he said at last, "that I don't know whether or not God wants me to marry. The answer to that depends on you." He looked up and met her eyes. "Because you're the person I want to marry, Dorrie."

She watched the warm blood stain his ears and high cheekbones, and she smiled. His dark eyes studied her face, but he did not return her smile. When he spoke again, his voice was very soft. "I love you, Dorrie Carpenter. How do you feel about me?"

She reached out her free hand and traced the strong lines of his brows and cheeks and nose. He closed his eyes, his face very still, as though he was afraid that if he moved, he would scare her hand away. "Don't you know by now?" she asked. "Can't you read it in my face?"

His mouth curved a little. "I think I can. But I need to hear the words."

She touched his dark hair, then tugged one of the wiry

curls until his face came closer to her own. "I'm through making up my own stories about what the future holds. But I hope very much that God does want you to marry." She smiled into his eyes, though for some reason she felt tears pricking beneath her lids. "Because I love you too, Alec MacIntyre."

"Dorrie," he said and sighed as though he had been holding his breath. His arms went around her. She closed her eyes and felt his warm mouth against her own.

&

After Alec said goodbye at last, Dorrie went inside. Clem and Mason were chaperoning a youth party at the church, and the little house was quiet and empty. Dorrie picked up her briefcase and sat down at the kitchen table to work on the next week's lessons. Her class was a source of joy to her, but they were also a constant challenge; no matter how excited she felt about her growing relationship with Alec, she knew she could not afford to neglect her responsibility to her students.

As she worked, she felt the stillness touching her, like a warm and gentle hand. Verse from Isaiah 32 came into her head: "And the work of righteousness shall be peace; and the effect of righteousness quietness and assurance forever. And my people shall dwell in a peaceful home, and in sure dwellings, and in quiet resting places." She smiled. The quiet that she had sensed all along in this little house no longer made her uneasy; she knew now that it was God's presence. At last, her heart could hear His quiet voice.

A Letter To Our Readers

Dear Reader:

In order that we might better contribute to your reading enjoyment, we would appreciate your taking a few minutes to respond to the following questions. When completed, please return to the following:

> Rebecca Germany, Editor
> Heartsong Presents
> P.O. Box 719
> Uhrichsville, Ohio 44683

1. Did you enjoy reading *The Quiet Heart*?
   - ❏ Very much. I would like to see more books by this author!
   - ❏ Moderately
     I would have enjoyed it more if _____

   _____

2. Are you a member of *Heartsong Presents*? Yes   No
   If no, where did you purchase this book? _____

   _____

3. What influenced your decision to purchase this book? (Check those that apply.)

❏ Cover	❏ Back cover copy
❏ Title	❏ Friends
❏ Publicity	❏ Other _____

4. On a scale from 1 (poor) to 10 (superior), please rate the following elements.

___Heroine   ___Plot

___Hero   ___Inspirational theme

___Setting   ___Secondary characters

5. What settings would you like to see covered in *Heartsong Presents* books?

_____

_____

6. What are some inspirational themes you would like to see treated in future books?_____

_____

_____

7. Would you be interested in reading other *Heartsong Presents* titles?   ❏ Yes   ❏ No

8. Please check your age range:
❏ Under 18   ❏ 18-24   ❏ 25-34
❏ 35-45   ❏ 46-55   ❏ Over 55

9. How many hours per week do you read? —————

Name _____

Occupation _____

Address _____

City _____ State _____ Zip _____

Don't miss these favorite Heartsong Presents *titles by some of our most distinguished authors!*
(*Voted favorites by our readers in a recent poll.*)

Your price is only $2.95 each!

___HP59 EYES OF THE HEART, *Maryn Langer*
___HP62 THE WILLING HEART, *Janelle Jamison*
___HP66 AUTUMN LOVE, *Ann Bell**
___HP70 A NEW SONG, *Kathleen Yapp**
___HP76 HEARTBREAK TRAIL, *VeraLee Wiggins*
___HP78 A SIGN OF LOVE, *Veda Boyd Jones**
___HP81 BETTER THAN FRIENDS, *Sally Laity**
___HP82 SOUTHERN GENTLEMAN, *Yvonne Lehman**
___HP83 MARTHA MY OWN, *VeraLee Wiggins*
___HP84 HEART'S DESIRE, *Paige Winship Dooley*
___HP85 LAMP IN DARKNESS, *Connie Loraine**
___HP86 POCKETFUL OF LOVE, *Loree Lough**
___HP87 SIGN OF THE BOW, *Kay Cornelius*
___HP88 BEYOND TODAY, *Janelle Jamison*
___HP90 CATER TO A WHIM, *Norma Jean Lutz**
___HP92 ABRAM MY LOVE, *VeraLee Wiggins*

*contemporary title

....Hearts ♥ng ....

... Presents ....

Great Inspirational Romance at a Great Price!

eartsong Presents books are inspirational romances in contempo-
ary and historical settings, designed to give you an enjoyable, spirit-
fting reading experience. You can choose from 116 wonderfully
ritten titles from some of today's best authors like Colleen L. Reece,
renda Bancroft, Janelle Jamison, and many others.

When ordering quantities less than twelve, above titles are $2.95 each.

SEND TO: Heartsong Presents Reader's Service
P.O. Box 719, Uhrichsville, Ohio 44683

Please send me the items checked above. I am enclosing $ _____
(please add $1.00 to cover postage per order. OH add 6.25% tax. NJ
add 6%.). Send check or money order, no cash or C.O.D.s, please.
To place a credit card order, call 1-800-847-8270.

NAME _____

ADDRESS _____

CITY/STATE _____ ZIP _____

HPS MARCH

Heartsong Presents
Love Stories Are Rated G!

That's for godly, gratifying, and of course, great! If you love a thrilling love story, but don't appreciate the sordidness of popular paperback romances, **Heartsong Presents** is for you. In fact, **Heartsong Presents** is the *only inspirational romance book club*, the only one featuring love stories where Christian faith is the primary ingredient in a marriage relationship.

Sign up today to receive your first set of four, never before published Christian romances. Send no money now; you will receive a bill with the first shipment. You may cancel at any time without obligation, and if you aren't completely satisfied with any selection, you may return the books for an immediate refund.

Imagine. . .four new romances every month—two historical, two contemporary—with men and women like you who long to meet the one God has chosen as the love of their lives. . .all for the low price of $9.97 postpaid.

To join, simply complete the coupon below and mail to the address provided. **Heartsong Presents** romances are rated G for another reason: They'll arrive *Godspeed!*